Evading

the Gentleman

WENDY MAY ANDREWS

☙❧

Sparrow Ink
www.sparrowdeck.com

ISBN - 978-1-989634-50-9

www.wendymayandrews.com

Stay in touch with Wendy May Andrews and forthcoming publishing news.

Sign up for her biweekly newsletter

She'll help with his investigation, but she'll *never* fall for him. Not again, anyway...

Daisy Alcott lost faith in love *long* ago. She has no patience for such nonsense. But that doesn't mean she'll never find a husband. She'll eventually marry and settle into a nice, loveless relationship where there's *zero* chance of getting hurt. Nothing will deter her from her plan. *Especially* not her childhood enemy—the boy next door who taught her *all* about heartbreak.

Foster Northcott has no time for courtship. He's been too busy trying to match his brother's success to even *consider* such matters. But when he finds himself caught up in a smuggling investigation that throws him into a partnership with the lovely Daisy, he starts to question every decision he's ever made. *Especially* the ones that kept him far from her for so long.

It will take more than a shared desire to capture some criminals to convince *this* pair of opposites to give romance a second chance. But as Daisy and Foster will soon learn, evading happily ever after is a *lot* harder than one might think...

Evading the Gentleman is a sweet and clean standalone Regency romance with perfect chemistry, memorable characters, a hint of intrigue, and a satisfying happy ending.

Dedication

Daisy is determined to make her way in life on her own terms, how she thinks will be best. She might have been wrong about what was best, but she'll find her way eventually. This book is for everyone trying to figure it out. And to my nieces who are all also on that journey of discovery. Love you ladies!

Acknowledgements

Acknowledgment number one has to go to my best friend and life partner, Mr. Andrews. Thank you for putting up with all the pizzas while this one got sorted. Thank you too for knowing and caring about my Northcotts nearly as much as I do. You're the best walking and talking partner a gal could ask for.

Acknowledgment number two must go to my parents. You two have always stood by me and supported me in all my endeavors. Thank you for loving my books and cheering me on. Thanks too for reading to me as a small child. I blame you for my love of words.

Aunt Marlene, I still miss you. Thanks for introducing me to Regencies – the love affair continues. Thankfully your daughter is nearly as good as you at pointing out where the stories can improve.

My beta readers – Alfred, Monique, Suzanne, and Christina – thank you so much for cheering for me, finding the plot holes, and making such fabulous suggestions where needed.

My gorgeous cover is thanks to the artistry of *Envision Literary Photography* and Les at *GermanCreative*. I'm thrilled with my beautiful covers in this series.

My editing team, Bev Rosenbaum and Julie Sherwood, are experts in their field. I am grateful for their input. The characters' goals and motivations have certainly deepened with their help as well as ironing out the kinks in this story, and putting in all the commas that I always leave lying about. Any remaining mistakes are entirely the fault of the author.

Chapter One

1800

Miss Daisy Alcott felt old. It was a ridiculous feeling for someone who had just achieved her twenty-second year, but there you had it – feelings didn't always make sense or follow any sort of logical course. But the amount of giggling she could hear throughout the crowded ballroom made her very aware of the fact that many of the other young women available on the Marriage Mart were much younger than she was.

And Daisy didn't feel much like giggling. The matter was far too serious.

Her sisters had certainly made their debuts at a younger age than she was. But of course, Daisy was no longer a debutante. She had made her first curtsy to the Queen several years ago. However, her family had been in mourning the past few years for various beloved family members and now here she was, getting a little long in the tooth, and still no husband and certainly no children on the way. Unlike her two sisters who delighted to write her long, effusive letters about all the joyous antics of their growing broods of children.

Daisy actually did love to hear from her sisters and loved her little nieces and nephews and was usually quite diverted by the tales of their adventures. But there were times, like right that moment, when she wished she was cradling a babe of her own, already established on the course of her adult life, rather than standing on the edge of a dance floor pondering which gentleman would be the best father for said future babe.

"That sigh was out of place on such a festive occasion."

Daisy nearly jumped from surprise and guilt when the deep voice came over her shoulder, but she was too busy fighting the shiver that threatened to make itself evident. She would not shiver over Foster Northcott.

"Frost," she said with as little inflection as possible, using the nickname they had all adopted as children for the middle son of the estate next door. "What are you doing here? I thought you were on the other side of the Atlantic."

"Shouldn't that be Mr. Northcott to such a young miss as yourself?"

Daisy's lips twitched, but she refused to allow the man beside her to think she was relenting in her determination to ignore him and his effect on her.

Foster Northcott was the bane of her existence.

With a roll of her eyes and another deep sigh, if one were to ask Daisy, she would readily admit that claiming someone to be a bane was rather more melodramatic than she was wont to be, especially at her ripe age, but he never failed to put her teeth on edge.

It had all started as a lark. They had actually played together as children. Daisy's brothers were friends with Foster Northcott and *his* brothers. Since Daisy's home, Alcott House, wasn't terribly far from Everleigh, there had been plenty of visiting back and forth amongst the boys. Daisy, of course, had never been to Everleigh, as it was an all-male establishment, but the Northcott boys had spent plenty of time at Alcott.

In an effort to remain conciliatory, at least in public, Daisy didn't snarl at him the way she would truly like to do. She tried to keep her antipathy under wraps and instead asked him what she thought would be a polite question.

"Have you heard from Ashford?"

"You know he's not going to come home and save you from spinsterhood, don't you?"

"Frost, do try not to be a worse dolt than necessary. It was merely a question as to his well-being. If you can't help yourself from being beastly, do take yourself off to some other section of the room."

Studiously maintaining her focused gaze on the musicians as they tuned their instruments during the break in dancing, Daisy refused to look at the handsome, annoying gentleman at her side.

"Why have you been left unattended? Shouldn't your mother or Florent, or even Reed, be by your side?"

"I'm not an invalid, Frost. I don't need my brothers or my mother to play nursemaid for me. Nor am I likely to get up to any sort of scandalous behavior standing here in a crowded ballroom. Or rather, I wasn't until you came to pester me. Now there might be some scandalous violence erupting any moment."

The rich chuckle that followed her pleasant but coolly toned statement would have melted a lesser woman's resistance, but not Daisy. She slowly turned her head and tried to sear the man with her glare.

"Do step away, Foster. I haven't the nerves for you tonight."

She shouldn't have said it. His gaze instantly sharpened. Daisy had noticed that he often couldn't meet her gaze, no doubt due to guilt from their past, but now she felt as though he were scouring her soul with his eyes.

"Why not? What's special about tonight?"

"Just go away," she finally snapped in lieu of a proper response. She was tired and cranky and had no patience for the frustratingly handsome gentleman.

"We did get a letter from Ash not that long ago. It was weeks old, of course, but he sounded to be well and hearty. I think he's actually much better there than here."

"Why, Foster Northcott, I do think you are jealous."

"Jealous of a brother who went off to sea at fifteen years of age and hasn't been seen in nearly a decade? Hardly."

Daisy could hear that he was trying to scoff, but it wasn't coming across sufficiently truthful.

With a frown, Daisy asked: "Do you wish they had taken you with them?"

"Hardly," he repeated, but there was no heat in it this time. "I couldn't have left my youngest brother behind, unlike Ash who didn't seem to have a care for any of us. Besides, I was almost seventeen. I couldn't possibly hang off my younger brother's coattails. But I have every intention of besting him all the same."

Her frown didn't disappear as she studied the handsome face at her side. He wouldn't meet her gaze, and she was reasonably sure he was trying to appear unconcerned with her study of his profile. She really wanted to ask him about his last statement but knowing sibling rivalry like she witnessed with her own brothers, she thought it wise not to dig into that morass in the crowded ballroom.

"Do you think you would have liked life at sea?" She knew her nose was wrinkling in distaste but didn't bother to curb her expression.

Foster shrugged. "Probably not. I didn't love the crossings I've endured, travelling back and forth to America. I cannot imagine spending any more time than necessary on a boat."

"Speaking of which, you didn't answer my question. What are you doing here? The last I heard from your sisters-in-law you weren't expected for weeks yet."

"Holding out for information about me, are you, Daisy?" His grin betrayed his rakish ways, but Daisy ignored it, instead offering him a shrug that mirrored the one he had sent her.

"They both dearly love sharing all the news of their families."

Foster nodded. "Isn't it odd that you're such good friends with both of them?"

"Why odd? We did make our debut together."

"But they are now married and starting their families."

"That doesn't change the fact that they are my friends. Do you intend to give up all your friends if you ever wed?"

"I have no intention of ever marrying, so it's a moot question."

"Then I will ask you once more, Frost, please leave off." She sighed lightly. "I *do* wish to wed, and your standing here beside me shan't help me in the least."

"Actually, it might help you," he countered with a grin. "I am known to be a connoisseur of womanly attractions."

Daisy rolled her eyes and then tried to whither him with her disdain. "I am not that sort of female, Frost. Your attention will do the opposite of helping me, I can assure you."

Foster clutched his chest in a mocking manner. "You wound me, dearest Daisy." He laughed and the rich, deep sound did inexplicable things to her midsection. "Point me in the direction of your brothers, and I'll leave you to your husband hunt, if you're going to be so weak-willed that you can't bandy words with one of your oldest friends for even a moment."

Gritting her teeth, Daisy managed to hold in all the various words that threatened to spill out in response. He was not her friend. With their five-year age difference, he had never truly been her friend. But ever since he had left her to drown that ill-fated summer day ten years before, she had truly loathed him with the single-minded focus that could only come about after having hung her youthful devotion upon his unsuspecting head.

He had always been the handsomest male she had ever seen, even as a boy, when she had barely realized what being a boy meant. But she had loved him deeply until he had laughed as she floundered in the water that day, when her newly acquired heavy skirts had weighed her down far more than she could have ever expected when she had jumped into the lake to save the bag of kittens someone had left to drown.

It didn't matter to her that he had always claimed that he hadn't realized she was struggling. Frost had also said he didn't realize how deep the water was, but Daisy had never believed him. Surely, he must have swum there often with her brothers, whether she had seen him or not. The fact that he had occasionally appeared anguished when the topic had arisen and that he had never looked her in the eye since told her he was lying. The other inconvenient fact, the one that told her he still had a hold on her heart, made her even more furious.

Her brother's arrival had saved both Daisy and the kittens that day, but she had never forgiven Frost for not saving her himself. If he had been the hero she had thought him, he surely would have risked himself for her. She knew it was irrational of her to blame him for her near-death experience. She had been the foolish one who had jumped into the cold lake without ever having learned to swim. In her defence, she hadn't expected it to be so deep. It had never occurred to her not to react to the need she had witnessed, nor had she thought others wouldn't react similarly.

It had been a learning moment for her, that was for certain. She had been aware from that moment on that she didn't necessarily think like other people, and she couldn't expect them to react the way she would. She ought to be grateful to Foster Northcott for that lesson. But she had never forgiven him for it and didn't see that she ever would. It was just too bad he happened to be related by marriage to two of her dearest friends.

"Have you accepted Amelia's invitation to her first house party? She is determined to bring Everleigh into fashion."

"Had the earldom ever gone out of fashion?" Daisy didn't want to discuss the invitation with Foster.

He lifted his shoulder in a negligent shrug. "Amelia would like to think so. It's more a matter of never entertaining. Since our mother died so many years ago, Everleigh hasn't hosted a single event. Amelia has every intention of changing that despite the fact that she claims to be averse to Society. Strange woman, but we quite like her."

Daisy couldn't help laughing at that.

"I suppose you're just getting to know her now, aren't you? So again, I must ask, what are you doing *here*? If you've just returned from America, shouldn't you be at Everleigh with your family?"

Foster's grin was nearly blinding, forcing Daisy to avert her gaze once more lest the beastly man see what his appearance did to her.

"I did spend some time there, but it reminded me how much I enjoy being elsewhere."

Despite her determination to remain cold to Foster Northcott, Daisy couldn't help feeling some sympathy for him. Since he left his home, there had been many changes to it and it couldn't be easy to settle in after so many years. She knew how frustrated she was with her own current state of feeling stuck between two life stages, it was likely he was in a similar circumstance.

"And so, you decided to come check out the Marriage Mart?" She had to bite back a grin as she heard the scepticism in her tone.

"It does seem quite out of character, doesn't it?" he returned with another wide smile that appeared forced to Daisy, but she might be reading things that weren't actually there. "But I didn't exactly come for the Mart. I just happened to come to Town and there were invitations at the house, so I accepted this one. The alternative was sitting around with the servants, and that didn't appeal to me."

"Of course not," she acknowledged. "Will you be in Town long?"

Again, he lifted a shoulder as though to indicate indifference or uncertainty. "I'm not sure. I'm at a bit of a crossroads at the moment. I will be looking into a few things here and there."

He was as maddening as ever, Daisy could see. She really shouldn't be engaging him in any conversation. If she held her silence, perhaps he would go. Before she could suit thought to action, or perhaps inaction, though, he asked her one more question.

"I say, Daisy, I know you said you don't need them, but aren't any of your brothers here to keep an eye out for you? Or one of your parents? I know you think you're an aging spinster, but surely someone ought to be watching over you anyway."

It took every ounce of her willpower to keep her words between her teeth and a snarl off her face. Foster Northcott never failed to bring out the worst in her. Daisy had always considered herself to be a fairly even-tempered person but in Frost's presence, she could be counted on to turn into a veritable raving lunatic. It was disconcerting even to her. She was more than relieved when Reed finally turned up at her elbow.

"Frost! What a lark. No one told me you'd be here. What are you doing looking over the dance floor like a fortune hunter? Come along to the refreshment table and tell me about your latest travels."

Daisy was thrilled that they'd both be gone. She loved her brothers but wasn't prepared to endure their presence while she was making such an important decision about her life. She only hoped any aging relatives stayed healthy enough this time that she could get the matter taken care of without interruption. Dismissing the two men by her side from her mind, she cast her gaze around the ballroom once more. And was thus very surprised by Foster's next words.

"I don't know, Reed. Ought we to leave Daisy on her own? It doesn't seem right to leave her unattended."

Daisy's lips twitched when a quick glance at her brother showed that his face mirrored the incredulity she could feel stamped upon her own.

"What's going to happen to her here? Surely, it's the safest place anyone could possibly imagine, at least for a marriage-minded girl. For bachelors such as ourselves it's probably exceedingly dangerous, but nothing could happen to Daisy. And you've known her since she was in the cradle. Surely you remember she can look after herself quite well."

Daisy appreciated her brother's confidence in her even if it might be slightly misplaced. And she did hope they hurried along. In her estimation, she was better off arranging these matters for herself without the input of any of her family members. Which was why she had managed to convince her mother she could spend her time with her cronies rather than standing attendance with Daisy. Since she had already been introduced to everyone during her abbreviated first Season, she didn't really need a nursemaid for this business. And it was her life, no one else's.

Chapter Two

Foster tried not to watch. He had given her some advice, and it appeared she was trying to follow it. With their past, he hadn't actually expected her to listen to him, but no one could claim she was stupid; she knew what was good for her.

He was happy for her; he truly was. He certainly had no interest in derailing her success. He was happy for her, he repeated to himself. And Daisy Alcott was not for him. No woman was for him at this point. He still had his fortune to amass.

Perhaps if he repeated it to himself often enough, he would believe it.

It was just being back in London. It never failed to turn his head. This was why he never did so on the rare occasion that he visited his home country. He was still needed in Upper Canada. Letters certainly were insufficient for conducting business. And he needed to arrange a few things in New York, too. It was unfortunate that he could not be in both places at once, and home at the same time. He was just fortunate that the ocean crossings were becoming faster and safer. In another couple of years, perhaps he would be in a position to pursue one of these women for himself. Well, probably not one of these exact ladies, as they would all surely be wed. But one of their sisters or cousins would become his life's partner.

It would have been nice if Daisy had an available sister. He would have liked to have aligned himself with the Alcott family.

That might be too strange, he acknowledged. How awkward to have complicated feelings for your sister-in-law. No, he couldn't even be thinking along these lines for a couple years yet.

Perhaps he would find a suitable woman in Canada. That might be better. But then it was likely she wouldn't want to come back to England with him.

Foster sighed. Dividing oneself between two places was a sort of ruination of one's sanity, it would seem. Nowhere was home now. He was always restless. He hoped that would fade once he reached the level of success he was after. Sometimes, though, he feared that he would always feel the need to strive for more. Especially if Ashford kept getting richer.

Perhaps he ought to forget about competing with his brother.

That errant thought almost made him chuckle out loud. He couldn't get himself clapped into Bedlam for laughing at nothing. He had too many things to accomplish.

Watching Daisy follow Merton through the steps of the dance so skillfully was making him daft. He certainly shouldn't follow them through to the supper room. And yet that was exactly what he did. And then he found a seat near enough to them that he could eavesdrop. There was no discernible reason for his ridiculous behavior. Merton wasn't involved in any of the reasons why Foster was in Town. This was doing nothing except addling his mind. Still, he sat there and strained his ears.

"Have you been in Town long?"

He almost hissed. She shouldn't let the gentleman know she hadn't been keeping track of him. Or perhaps she should. He had told her to let the gentlemen chase after her, not the other way around. It would seem she was following his instructions. Because surely every young lady knew when the highly eligible gentlemen arrived in Town. Especially intelligent, marriage-minded young women like Daisy.

But she was also honest, sometimes to a fault, so he reckoned perhaps she actually hadn't taken note of when Merton had arrived. Foster grimaced and continued to listen.

"Not terribly long. I missed the opening sessions in the House as there were poor roads in my county."

There was a brief pause while Foster watched Daisy stare at Merton.

"Did you stay behind to repair them?" Her forehead was wrinkled in adorable confusion.

Foster nearly snorted even while trying not to appear as though he were listening. Eavesdropping had never been his forte. He was much better at getting his answers through strategic questioning, face-to-face. But he still couldn't stop himself. It was almost a compulsion. He awaited Merton's reply along with Daisy, wondering if the man would scoff at her question or answer her reasonably.

To his surprise, the viscount sounded as though he were smiling when he finally answered her. "You would have loved to think of me with a shovel in my hand, wouldn't you? But I can assure you that road work is far more heavy than gardening."

"So, was that a yes or a no?" she countered with a dry chuckle.

"I admit, I didn't do much of the labor myself. But I stayed behind to ensure it was completed."

"No doubt your neighbours were pleased with you."

Now Merton surprised Foster further by laughing. "To be honest, they would have been happier if I had paid attention to the state of the roads earlier rather than waiting until my own need for them made me realize what a state they were in."

"Now I'm curious." Daisy didn't seem appalled by his lack of maintenance work attention. "Have you not left your estate in that long or did something dreadful happen to destroy the roads in the meantime?"

Foster realized he was being beyond ridiculous, bordering on insanity. He couldn't sit around listening in on this conversation. Daisy was not his responsibility. In fact, even her brothers were not claiming any responsibility toward watching over the grown woman. He ought to respect her enough to allow her a degree of privacy. And he truly had no reason to think Lord Merton would harm her in any way. While the viscount might not be quite as sterling as other eligible gentlemen, he was irreproachable, and Foster was being beyond foolish for wishing to interfere somehow.

It was particularly ridiculous since he had given Daisy the suggestions that had no doubt resulted in this encounter. And he wasn't about to court her himself. So, he ought to be happy for her rather than hovering around like an anxious mother.

He was neither anxious nor a mother. He was an eligible bachelor on a mission. Multiple missions to be frank. He shouldn't have even attended the ball that night except that he had been filled with such restlessness that he couldn't bear to remain at his family's townhouse for the evening. But now it called to him. Perhaps a night of solid sleep would settle him. He hadn't slept well for the week since he'd been off the boat. It was always an adjustment being back on land after having been rocked to sleep by the sea every night for the past many weeks.

***

He was awakened by increasingly loud knocking.

14

"Mr. Northcott, why is this door barred?"

Foster sighed. It was a habit borne of living in unfamiliar surroundings for the last several years.

"One moment." Quickly gaining his wits, Foster hopped out of bed, refreshed from the long night of solid sleep.

"My apologies. I hadn't wished to be disturbed," he excused and accused all at once. There was really no reason why any of the servants should have need of him that morning. His locked door shouldn't have been a problem to anyone.

"There is a gentleman to see you."

"There is? Who is it?"

"Mr. Reed Alcott, sir."

Foster groaned even as he began donning his clothes. "I will be a few minutes. Please, let him know he can either wait for me or return later. We didn't have an appointment."

He hadn't bothered to take his leave of his friend the night before. When he had realized he was being such a fool over Daisy, he had left the ball immediately, barely stopping to take his leave of his hostess. He certainly hadn't wanted to dither around giving his friends explanations. Besides, Foster had known that Reed would have insisted he go to a club or some other extravagant carousing that he had no use for. But surely that wasn't why the man was calling so early.

"What is wrong with you that you are such a slugabed on this fine day?" Reed greeted him when Foster appeared in the breakfast room where Reed had been shown.

"It's not that late, Reed. I'd be surprised if you've even been to bed yet."

"I'll sleep when I'm dead," the other man declared with a flourish as he brought a cup of strong coffee to his grinning mouth. "I'm surprised you would bother to waste any of your time with sleep. Don't you have a brother to beat to the highest pile of gold coins?"

Foster laughed. "Some of us mortals realize that we are much more successful when rested. You'd better not have drunk all my coffee. I have a feeling I'm going to need it if I'm to be spending time with you this morning." He suited his words to actions, filling his plate from the sideboard and accepting a steaming cup of coffee from the attentive footman. "Now tell me, Reed, what has brought you by in such a tizzy that you had to make our footman disturb my sleep."

"From what I heard, it was the locked door that was the problem, not my arrival."

Foster blinked. He would have expected Everleigh servants to have a touch more discretion.

"Don't look so appalled, Frost," Reed carried on with a chuckle. "It wasn't trade secrets. I overheard the footman telling the butler. You know I've always had the hearing of a cat."

"What can I do for you, Reed?" There was no use making an incident out of it. It would only cause more questions in his friend's mind.

"You aren't going off to this house party, are you? A few of us were thinking of going to find some sport, perhaps fishing or hunting or maybe some sailing."

"I just got off a boat, Reed," Foster said with a drawl. "And I also only just met my new sister-in-law. I'm not likely to keep my position as her favorite new brother if I don't show up to the event."

"She'll understand; she has brothers."

"It doesn't matter, Reed. I've only just arrived. I cannot go traipsing off elsewhere for sport at a time like this. I won't be staying long. It would be beyond the pale if I didn't attend."

"Well, you're not at home now; you're up in London. So how is this any different?"

Foster shook his head over his old friend's ignorance. "If you are that much pining for my company, Reed, then accept the invitation to Everleigh."

"I've already made the arrangements with my friends."

"But you don't even know which you would be doing," Foster reasoned with a frown. "You said hunting or fishing or maybe sailing. So, it doesn't sound like such firm plans. Tell me what the real issue is."

"I don't want to be match made by your sister," Reed finally blurted the words. "I just got my estate. I know I'm a catch now. But I'm not ready. I want to bask in my bachelorhood for a bit longer. And really, the property's not entailed or tied to some long legacy, so I needn't ever marry if I haven't a mind to do so."

Foster finally laughed. It felt good, as though he were releasing long pent-up tension. He might not have the same life experiences as Reed Alcott these days, but he was well reminded of the good friends they'd been as boys. It was nice to be back for a time.

"I have no intention of allowing my new sisters to match me either, even if that were their intention. But I have to be there, regardless of that."

Reed didn't look convinced, but he didn't argue further.

"Very well, Frost, if you're going to be disagreeable," he began, trying to sound fierce and disapproving, but he couldn't hold onto it and started laughing halfway through his bluster. "Never mind, I suppose I understand. Family is family. But are you busy today? Could we go riding or to the club or something? I have a feeling you shan't be around for long."

"You aren't wrong on that, Reed. I have to get back to Canada. There were just a few things I needed to take care of here."

"You travelled all the way back here just to take care of a few things? Are you daft?"

Foster laughed as he drank the last of his coffee. "Your sister asked me the same thing last night. I would like to think I'm not. But perhaps if you both think so, there might be some truth to it."

Reed joined him in laughter. "Do you like the ocean crossing that much that you would do it frequently?"

"Not in the least. It can really be quite dreadful. This time wasn't bad. It seems to be the season for it. So, I'd like to wrap up my business and set out again in the hopes that it stays pleasant."

Reed appeared sceptical and Foster tried not to allow it to affect him. Perhaps it had been impetuous to come home, but it wasn't as frivolous as he had implied. It had been two years since Lucian had married Amelia. They had survived not meeting in person in all that time. But this time, there was something pressing Gilbert asked him to look into at Everleigh when Foster had mentioned he might come home for a time. Something Gilbert didn't wish to involve Lucian in. Foster returning would provide the distraction Gilbert needed to be able to dig into it further. And Frost could help. As soon as he had read Gilbert's letter, he had booked the next crossing. It might seem impetuous, but it wasn't a bad thing. He had needed to come back to England anyway. Gilbert's letter had just solidified his plans. It would all work out just fine.

And he got to meet his new sisters. Altogether it was going to be a great time, even if it was unusually short by many people's standards.

"You can watch out for my sister while you're there, then, I suppose."

"I thought you didn't consider her in need of watching over."

"Not in a ballroom," Reed scoffed. "But I would think a house party is a completely different matter."

"Your mother will surely accompany her," Foster began before realizing he ought to be insulted on his family's behalf. "Besides, what do you think would possibly happen to her at Everleigh?"

Reed shrugged. "Daisy knows how to find trouble. And our mother has become lax. I suspect it has something to do with having escorted two others before Daisy. It was a smooth arrangement with both of the other girls. But Daisy is an entirely different matter. She thinks she's fully grown and nearly on the shelf, so she intends to arrange her own match without input from the rest of the family. The girl is just looking for trouble if you ask me."

"Did she ask you?"

Reed laughed. "Of course not. But I care about my sister. Not enough to bestir myself, of course. But enough to suggest if you're there, too, you might as well keep an eye out for her."

Foster felt a curl of anger unfurl in his stomach. Poor Daisy's family was nearly as uninvolved in her life as his was in his own. He resolved to do as Reed asked, which he would have done anyway as that was his nature. But he would make sure she didn't make a disastrous match. Not that his sisters would be inviting anyone disastrous to their party, but some matches were better than others, he was sure.

"Come along Reed, I have a few things to do today and then we can go riding or to the club or whatever you wish."

The younger man brightened as though he had been offered a rare treat.

"Really, Frost?" he asked as eager as a boy. "I thought perhaps you were far too busy and important for us indolent sots."

"We can be indolent after I've been busy," Foster agreed with a grin. He didn't give credence to Reed's sceptical expression, merely escorted him from the room.

Chapter Three

Daisy paced the foyer awaiting her mother. It was unusual that she was the one ready first. But she was full of conflicting feelings about the upcoming house party and hadn't been able to sleep. So now she was cooling her heels in the foyer impatiently awaiting the carriage being brought around and her mother to join her. It was very early in the morning, and they had a long day of travel ahead of them. She only hoped the roads were good. After Lord Merton's comments a few nights before, it was just one more thing for Daisy to be worrying about.

With a sigh of relief, she heard her mother coming.

"You are ready much earlier than I would have expected, Daisy. I thought I'd be awaiting you. My apologies if you have been dithering here a while. I should have had my maid check with yours."

"I haven't been here overlong. I was unable to sleep," she explained.

"Oh dear. Hopefully the long drive will allow you plenty of opportunity to nap. Or are you too agitated to do so?"

Despite their very different temperaments, Daisy's mother knew her well. She offered the older woman a smile.

"I have a feeling I'll fall instantly asleep as soon as we're on the way. It will be too late to change anything then, so the agitation might subside."

"Plus, the motion of the carriage might just rock you off to dreamland."

"I do hope so. It wouldn't do to arrive at Everleigh and yawn all through the first supper."

To Daisy's surprise her mother chuckled. "I strongly doubt you'll find yourself yawning while at Everleigh, no matter how tired you might be."

"Is it that overbearing that I'll be too intimidated to yawn?"

"Something like that. Not exactly. But you will see for yourself soon enough. But not if we don't hurry along. We can discuss it at length on the drive. Goodness knows we'll have the time."

As Daisy followed her mother into the carriage and they were tucked in with each of their maids facing them, she asked her mother, "Are you regretting having accepted the invitation?"

"Not in the least, why would you ask that?"

Daisy lifted an indecisive shoulder. "You seem to be dreading the drive."

"Well, of course I am. It'll be dreadful. But it will be worth the drive, I'm sure. And we'll have plenty of time to recover there. I do expect we will enjoy ourselves. It is merely the long drive that is a necessary evil. And truly, I shouldn't complain. Since the weather has been so dry, we should be able to make it in one day. It could have been much worse. And we might even be able to stop in to Alcott House at some point to see how the servants are. While I am certain the housekeeper would write if there was anything I ought to know about, I wouldn't mind to see with my own eyes that all is well at home."

Daisy nodded. It was a little strange to think of going visiting to a house in their own neighbourhood. She was anxious to get there. Because Lucian, Viscount Adelaide, had taken his new wife on a tour of all his father's properties almost immediately following their marriage trip, Daisy hadn't actually seen her friend, his wife, Lady Amelia, since they had debuted together. Of course, they had written frequently, but it would be so nice to see her again in the flesh. To be able to say all the things that went unsaid when writing.

But the long drive would certainly be a chore. And the worry about missed opportunities in Town. It was a trifle odd to be leaving Town at the height of the Season. But since no one had yet shown a marked interest in her, she probably wasn't about to miss much.

Daisy took a deep breath and counted to ten. She needed to change her train of thought. Or the tempo of her thoughts. She wasn't exactly certain how to phrase what she meant, but the direction of her thoughts was going the wrong way. Not that she believed she could will herself into an appropriate marriage, but she was reasonably sure she was willing it in the wrong way with her negativity.

She would find a good husband. Perhaps even at the house party. She knew Amelia would be beside herself with delight if she did and had therefore invited the most eligible gentlemen she could think of. It was a truly sweet gesture, if one thought about it in that light. Or it was the most meddlesome thing a friend could do. Daisy was determined to think of it in the positive light and will herself into a pleasing match.

Everyone would be happy with that outcome.

"You mustn't put such pressure on yourself, Daisy, dear." Once again, her mother had surprised her.

"Whatever do you mean?"

"There is no need for you to rush into marriage. You are the last daughter at home. I am in no rush to be rid of you. I know there have been disappointments with not being able to come up for the Season for a time, but I have grown quite accustomed to your companionship and your assistance at home. I will be saddened to see the back of you."

Daisy reached over and clasped her mother's hand. She thought that was quite the nicest thing her mother had ever said to her. But of course, she couldn't take her mother up on the offer. It was well past time for her to be getting on with her life. Still, it was a kindness. And perhaps Daisy ought to try to relieve some of the pressure she had been putting on the matter.

"Thank you, Mama. I do appreciate that. Perhaps I have grown too serious about this Marriage Mart business. But while it is kind of you to say I am welcome at home, I feel ready to have a home of my own. While I don't object to how we do things at Alcott, I'd like to figure out how I want to do things in my own home. And then there's the matter of children. Hearing about my nieces and nephews never fails to put a lump in my throat. I want to have those every day."

"That doesn't sound in the least bit comfortable," Mama countered drily.

Daisy laughed good naturedly but quickly sobered. "I'm certain you know what I'm talking about, Mama. I just want to get on with it."

"I know, dear. But try to enjoy it, too."

"I will. I appreciate the reminder. I had been questioning the wisdom of accepting this invitation even though it is from one of my dearest friends. Now I will forget all my questions and just enjoy the break from the whirl of the Season."

"I'm not certain a house party will be any less of a whirl," Mama countered.

"But we shan't have to drive anywhere to get to the whirl," Daisy concluded with a chuckle before lapsing back into her corner to watch the passing scenery.

"Do you know who all has been invited?"

"I do know who was invited but not necessarily who accepted the invitation."

"I expect it to be highly entertaining."

Daisy stared at her mother with elevated eyebrows causing a surprisingly girlish giggle to escape the older woman.

"Amelia Courtenay was an odd female for you to strike up a friendship with," she pointed out. "I am curious to see how she is making out as Viscountess Adelaide, the future Countess of Everleigh. Evidently, if the old earl is allowing her to throw this party, he has mellowed significantly since last I saw him."

"Which was when, Mama? I cannot recall ever meeting him, since I've never known of him leaving his estate, and we were never invited to visit."

"It was a bit strange that he never entertained at all, seeing as we were nearly neighbours. But grief does strange things to different people, and we cannot judge the poor man."

"Of course not. But I will admit to an intense amount of curiosity."

"That is fair. I too am eager to see how the fortnight shall progress."

"Fortnight? I thought we were only staying for a week."

"Is that all you packed for?"

Daisy laughed. "Well, no. A lady has to be prepared for all eventualities."

"Good girl." Mama's approval brought a different sort of lump into Daisy's throat. "It's true that the main party is planned for a week, but Amelia wrote to be prepared for longer in case we were having such a fine time that we wanted to remain a few more days. So, I only accepted invitations on a tentative basis back in Town just in case you wished to linger. Or even if we wished to stop in at home for a time."

"If, by some miracle, I manage to find my match at Everleigh, I would love to stop in at home. But I am not holding my breath on that eventuality."

"One should never hold their breath on things they have no control over, my dear," Lady Alcott murmured.

Daisy sighed. A part of her would love to return home, but that would not get her future sorted out, and that needed to remain her focus until it was concluded. She would not allow herself to be sidetracked by anything else. Independence was nearly within her grasp. She could not miss the opportunities, and they were certainly not to be found at Alcott.

"Is it strange to you to be visiting Everleigh after all these years?"

Daisy was determined not to be surprised by her own mother's insightful questions. She had known the woman all her life. She ought to know how insightful she was. It was beyond foolish to be surprised by it. And yet Daisy couldn't recall her mother ever asking her so many questions that got directly to the heart of her concerns.

"I will own to being curious to see it. And yes, the passage of time has developed a sort of mystique about the place. What's more strange is that my two friends, whom I have seen so little of since I debuted, will be there."

"I am sure that will be a highlight for you. Do try to enjoy it rather than forever having your focus on the gentlemen."

Heat suffused Daisy for a moment. She was uncertain if it was anger or embarrassment. Perhaps a combination of the two.

"Are you suggesting that I would indiscriminately pursue multiple gentlemen?"

"I would never suspect you of doing something so *déclassé*. But I am afraid that you will be so focused on your objective that you will fail to take advantage of the opportunity to enjoy time with your friends. Marriage is forever, my dear. An opportunity like this to see two of your dearest friends in the flesh is a rarity, especially with your determination to wed. Who knows where you'll be this time next year?"

Daisy wanted to harrumph, but there was a kernel of truth to her mother's words.

"Do you know? Foster said the very same thing two nights ago at the ball he attended with Reed."

"I was unaware that he attended with Reed. But I always knew he was an intelligent boy."

"That boy is a world travelling man now, Mama."

Lady Alcott's eyebrows rose as she glanced at her daughter. "Are you considering him a possible match?"

Daisy actually scoffed at her mother. "As if. Not after the stunt he pulled when we were children. I could never trust him after that. Not with my own life and certainly not with my children's."

"It was a long time ago, my dear. People can change considerably as they grow up."

Daisy lifted one shoulder as though to indicate indifference. "I believe one's character is formed quite early in life."

Daisy's mother didn't bother to argue, merely returning her gaze to the quickly passing scenery. Daisy followed her gaze and then was struck by another thought.

"Lord Merton mentioned that his roads were dreadful. That was what delayed him arriving in Town for the current Session. But these seem to be faultless. I didn't think Merton was so far out of the way that he would have very different conditions. Do you know where Merton is, Mama?"

"Perhaps his lordship's carriage isn't as well sprung as ours. Or it's possible his constitution isn't as strong as yours. But I do believe Merton is in the other direction from Town. More in the direction of Bath."

"I wonder if he takes the waters." She meant it as a jest, but then she lapsed into wondering about the famed architecture of Bath. Daisy had heard much about the recent construction taking place there but had not yet seen it for herself. She tapped her chin and wondered if the viscount had accepted Amelia's invitation. Daisy was certain he had been given one.

She grew more anxious to arrive at their destination, but Daisy willed herself to get some rest. It would put her on the wrong foot to arrive in a sleep deprived state of fog.

The remainder of the drive passed quickly as both ladies lapsed into sleep and their maids watched over them quietly.

A crick was in her neck when she awoke but that was quickly stretched out. Daisy could tell they were near their destination, as the passing scenery began to feel increasingly familiar. She turned to her maid for some last-minute adjustments to her hair and attire, brushing crumbs from her skirts that had fallen while eating their lunch, and twitching the wrinkles out of her sleeves.

It was a good thing they had made an effort to right their appearance. Someone must have been watching for their arrival as suddenly what appeared to be half the household had swarmed outside to greet them. There would be no waiting in the carriage for a comb to be brought to them, Daisy thought with a grin as she saw her two friends awaiting her.

There was much laughter and squealing as the three young women embraced and chattered all at once and over top of each other, but still they seemed to follow each conversational thread. The others watched indulgently for a moment before Viscount Adelaide stepped forward and righted the situation.

"My dear, do allow her ladyship to enter and get settled. Surely you can catch up further with Miss Alcott later."

Amelia quickly turned to Lady Alcott. "My deepest apologies, my lady. I promise this is not a foregleam of what your visit is to be like. It was just so exciting that my good sense got pushed out the window."

"No apologies necessary, my dear. I do have three daughters, so I am well aware of the delights of female companionship. It was a pleasure to behold."

"Thank you, my lady," Amelia replied with a glance under her eyelashes toward her husband.

Daisy intercepted the glance and wasn't sure if Amelia was trying to see if her husband was irritated with her or if she was defying him as though to say 'see, the lady didn't mind.' It took effort not to giggle over the silent exchange. Even though Daisy couldn't quite tell what her friend was expressing to her husband, it made her glad to see that they had reached a comfortable understanding.

While she didn't want a love match for herself, Daisy did hope to be comfortable with her future husband and come to feel a familial bond. She and her siblings had that sort of ability to communicate with a modicum of words and facial expressions. It was quite lovely when one thought about it.

She made a mental note that this was a requirement for her future mate. Not that she had any idea how she could know if he were capable of such. Perhaps if she could witness him with long-time friends or siblings that would give her a clue as to his abilities in that regard.

A glance at her mother reminded her of their conversation in the carriage. She wasn't here for the sole purpose of finding her husband. Daisy had accepted her mother's counsel that she ought to try to enjoy the house party as much for herself as for her husband hunt. And she had every intention of succeeding at both.

Threading her hands through her friends' elbows she allowed herself to be directed into the large building.

Daisy only hoped her chin didn't unhinge on her.

Everleigh was spectacular.

The Great Hall they were ushered into was aptly named. Sometimes these types of rooms were called great but weren't so very large. Not that Daisy had visited all that many country homes of other nobles, but in their townhouses, she had noticed the misnomers at times. This was not at all the case at Everleigh. In fact, they could have gone for an even grander name.

What could be grander than Great? Grand? Enormous? Stupendous? She supposed none of those would be appropriate, she thought with a sigh before calling herself to task for woolgathering. But in any case, Everleigh was a pleasure to behold.

Of course, as a youngster, she had seen it frequently from a distance. As a bachelor establishment following the death of the countess, Daisy was never permitted to visit, but as the largest estate in their part of the country, she had been consumed with curiosity as a child and had frequently ridden on the property, close enough to stare at the sprawling, imposing edifice. Even though she knew some of the sons, the entire estate seemed so mysterious to her. She had often fantasized about the various occupants, making up stories about its history and imagining what the interior might look like.

It did not disappoint.

The warm, red, sandstone of the outside was reflected in the massive foyer, and Daisy almost gulped at the magnitude of the large house. Meeting her friend's gaze caused Amelia to split her face with a grin. She was too well bred to actually laugh out loud, but it was evident to Daisy that Amelia had been waiting for just that reaction.

"Just a little bit of a hovel, isn't it?" Amelia whispered as they swept through the foyer without allowing Daisy to take it all in. "You have days on end to stare at all the details, Daisy dear. Let us show you to your room so you can take off your coat and boots and be comfortable."

"I'm not certain one can be comfortable in this sort of place," she whispered back.

"Don't be silly. I live here. You do get used to it; I promise."

"I don't think I'm staying long enough for that," Daisy insisted with a light laugh.

Daisy had met the two sisters-in-law, newly married into the Northcott family, Amelia and Caroline, when the three of them had made their debut two and a half years earlier. The three young women had stayed in touch through letters in the intervening time, but this was the first time they were seeing each other since Amelia and Caroline had each abruptly left Town upon their marriages. Daisy had thought she had prepared herself well for the meeting, but it was even better than she had anticipated.

"Tell us everything." Amelia and Caroline perched on the bed in the middle of the lovely, sun-filled room they had shown Daisy to. It was evident she was to be treated as a special guest during this sojourn in the country. Daisy doubted even her mother had such a fine room. Her heart swelled at the thoughtful gesture from her friends.

"Everything about what?" Daisy asked with a chuckle. "That's such a broad question. For example, I don't think you want to know everything about my drive to Everleigh as it was rather dull and uneventful."

"No, don't be silly." Amelia threw a pillow at Daisy while Caroline simply giggled.

"Tell us about your Season, you noddy." Daisy grinned at Caroline's mild insult.

"That too has been rather dull, if you must know," Daisy admitted. "Neither of you are there, for one thing. Which brings me to my gripe with the two of you. Why haven't either of you come up for the Season? I understand a little why you might not Caroline, since your husband doesn't have a Seat he must take, but my Lady Adelaide, why have you and your viscount not come for the sitting of the House?"

Amelia made a rather significant gesture toward her midsection causing squeals to spill from all three young women.

"Never say so." Daisy breathed even as she fought to swallow her jealousy. It was bad enough that her sisters were well along in their lives, but now her friends were leaving her behind as well.

"It's early yet, I didn't intend to announce it publicly until after the party, but I couldn't keep it from you, my dear friend. And I didn't want to tell you in a letter. It is part of why I planned this party."

"But you aren't even showing, really. Why did that prevent you from coming? Are you terribly ill?"

"Not terribly. I suspect Adelaide is averse to being in Town and used my increasing as an excuse. And I didn't mind, so I didn't argue. It isn't nearly as exciting when you're a matron as when you are a maiden, I wouldn't think." Amelia looked as though she believed the words she was saying. Daisy refused to accept them.

"I doubt that's true. There is far too much uncertainty when you are unwed. And it causes much too much anxiety."

"Whatever do you mean?" Caroline inquired with a frown. "Are you still a wallflower?"

Daisy nodded a little miserably but then lifted her chin as though in defiance.

"Tell us all," Caroline demanded.

After outlining to her friends what a failure she felt, they commiserated as kindly as they could for ladies who had found their love match within weeks of making their debut.

"I know it seems to you as though we couldn't possibly understand, but do trust that we can empathize if not fully sympathize. We know what being a wallflower felt like. And we can imagine that it must be particularly trying for you to be sharing the Season with far younger women when all you wish to do is get on with your life."

Daisy's eyes filled with tears at her friend's profound understanding. There was something so comforting about feeling as though someone could feel for her. Daisy squeezed Caroline's hand in thanks. "It's the uncertainty. I wouldn't mind waiting if I could know for certain that in six months or three months or even twelve months, the perfect gentleman would present himself to my father and ask for me to wed with him. But I don't know if anyone will ever come up to scratch. It has been dreadful. I haven't truly had the impression that anyone has taken that sort of interest in me, and it has been terribly disheartening."

"Well, that is where my house party comes in handy, then," Amelia countered bracingly. "We've invited all the most eligible gentlemen. You shall have your pick."

Daisy laughed. "It's not that simple, Amelia. I shan't be proposing to *them*."

Amelia dismissed her words with a lift of her shoulder. "You are an intelligent young woman. You will be able to get the one you want to ask you; I am certain of it. This week will allow you to see each of the candidates in the best light. Far better than merely meeting them at balls or the theatre. Here you will be able to actually get to know them. Just ask Caroline how successful a house party can be."

Caroline dipped her head and blushed even though it had already been two years since she had wed Gilbert Northcott.

"But you ladies do remember that I don't wish for a love match as you have both found, though, right?"

"I think you're daft, but I do remember that. All the more reason for you to make an informed choice about your spouse, no feelings need attach themselves. I would think that a house party and getting to know a fellow might be better for someone wishing to avoid love. At a ball where you are dancing and barely talking is far more likely to stir up the warmer feelings than when you can speak more freely."

Daisy wasn't sure if Amelia had a good point or not, but it really mattered very little. She had accepted the invitation and was to be there for at least the next se'en-night. It was sure to be a lark whether she found her husband or not. Her mother had been wise when she advised Daisy to stop worrying so much about it.

"Who has arrived thus far?"

"You and your mother were the first. We actually don't expect everyone to finish their arrivals until sometime tomorrow, to be honest. Most are coming from Town same as you did, but we wanted to make sure you were here before everyone else."

"Why?" Daisy frowned.

"So no one gets the jump on you," Amelia said as though Daisy were daft.

Daisy laughed. "It isn't as though you've invited anyone I haven't yet met, have you? There is no jump to be gotten. But you are a dear to have put so much thought and effort in trying to help me. I do truly appreciate it, even if I sound sceptical. I promise I shall do my very best to ensure we have success."

Caroline laughed, too. "I don't think it's supposed to take effort on your part, Daisy. You are to be cosseted and pampered and honored. We shall be putting in the effort as the hostesses."

"That won't do for me and surely you must know it."

Amelia patted her on the head as though she were a pet. "Do try, my dear." Daisy gritted her teeth, determined not to be angry with her friend for her condescension. "Now, hurry and do whatever needs doing. I cannot wait another minute before I show you everything. I promise you shall love Everleigh. And you'll love it even more once I've convinced my father-in-law to perform all the improvements I have recommended. I will show you them all."

Caroline and Daisy exchanged a glance. Amelia had always been the most managing female of Daisy's acquaintance.

"How is the earl taking your suggestions?"

"With a grumble and a pinch of salt," Amelia answered with a light laugh, not seemingly bothered in the least.

After the day of travelling, Daisy was relieved when the tour was finally called to an end by the need to assemble for an early supper.

"I hope you don't mind that we keep country hours here," Amelia excused when she returned Daisy to her room after Caroline left them to confer with the housekeeper.

"Not in the least. We are in the country. Besides, after the long drive, I won't be up for a late night tonight anyway."

"There's something so exhausting about travelling even if you do nothing, isn't there?" Amelia said by way of agreeing. "Will you be able to find your way down to the green room where we'll be meeting before going into the dining room?"

"I think so," Daisy answered promptly. "But if not, I did notice that you have a very large staff. I am certain one of your footmen will be able to point me in the right direction if I should get turned around."

Amelia smiled, nodded, and then impulsively pulled her friend into a hug.

"Thank you for coming," she whispered. "I know you weren't too keen on the idea. But I promise you won't regret it."

"Even if it comes to nothing, how could I regret a week of visiting with my two favourite friends?" Daisy countered lightly just before she shut her door on one of said friends. Leaning against the closed door she heaved a sigh of relief. She loved Amelia and Caroline dearly, but Daisy realized she had never spent such an extensive amount of time with either of the other women. There was going to be a certain level of emotional toll this week. She would need a good meal and then a long night of sleep to recover from the day and to be fortified for whatever the upcoming week might hold.

Chapter Four

Foster was impatiently waiting in the receiving room where Amelia had insisted was appropriate to assemble prior to the evening meal. He tugged at the neck of his shirt, irritated that his valet had tied his cravat too tight. He ought to have done it himself, but he had worried that he would be all thumbs that evening.

Since he had set out to amass his fortune as soon as he had finished school rather than taking a Grand Tour as did most of his friends, Foster didn't feel very adept socially. Certainly not within High Society. While the matrons of New York Society liked to make a fuss over him whenever he visited that fair city, and he did perfectly well in what passed for society in the wilds of Upper Canada, Frost had a feeling it was going to be very different here at Everleigh. Perhaps it was actually *because* it was at Everleigh that he was feeling such uncharacteristic nerves. It wasn't as though they had ever entertained in his lifetime, at least not in the lifetime he could remember. Lucian and Gilbert claimed to remember wondrous entertainments held when they were small, but Frost couldn't claim any such recollections. It also might be his nerves over pleasing his new sisters. One of whom would soon be the mistress of this great pile of stones that was their ancestral home.

Not that the earl was about to give up his earthly coil any time soon.

Foster had never seen his father so, he didn't want to say cheerful as that would be an overstatement, but perhaps just not dour. Was so not dour an acceptable expression? Most likely not. Once again, he tugged at his cravat. He was losing his mind.

And then there was a stir of activity outside the door to the receiving room and Foster's nerves ratcheted up another notch. The first of the guests had arrived that afternoon. Frost hadn't been prepared for the fact that Amelia had invited Daisy and her mother to arrive in advance of the other guests. It made sense in a convoluted female sort of way, but it just added to Foster's discomfort. They would have to be polite and sociable without a great deal of other guests to dilute any tensions. What could possibly go wrong?

He took one more tug at the neck of his shirt and then slipped into a practiced persona. He had learned how to fake his way through whatever discomfort he might be facing long ago. First in school when the teachers wanted to compare him to his older brothers, then when he landed in the colonies determined to make his fortune.

Being the middle of five brothers had certainly prepared him well for what was to come. He could stand out or blend in no matter what the circumstances called for. Surely a supper with an eligible female and her very marriage-minded mama would be easy to endure. It couldn't possibly be as bad as facing bears or wolves as he had in Canada that one time.

A practiced smile was pinned to his face when he stepped forward to greet Lady Alcott and her daughter. He made every effort to keep his reaction under control. Foster had never seen Daisy looking so well. He bowed over each of their hands with a brief kiss to the wrist. Lady Alcott tittered like a school girl, much to the amusement of all in the room. Unlike her mother, Daisy twitched as though she wished to pull her hand out of his but other than that showed no reaction at all.

Interesting.

He hadn't remembered her having such control over herself. He supposed much had changed in the many years since they'd last spent much time together, other than that one recent ball in Town. He too had gained full control over himself. Which he proceeded to demonstrate by smiling politely and walking away from the lovely young woman without a backward glance.

Blessedly, they hadn't long to wait before the butler announced the evening meal, and there was a bustle of activity as they made their way to the small dining room.

They were eating in family style that evening as it was only the earl, his firstborn son, the viscount's wife, Gilbert, Gilbert's wife, Foster, and Roderick besides the two early arrivals. Since they weren't quite evenly numbered and nearly all related, Amelia declared free run of the house that evening. Everyone could sit wherever they'd like.

Foster found himself across the table from Daisy, who was squeezed in between her two friends. Amelia was at the foot of the table, looking to all appearances as though she were completely comfortable there until Frost noticed a slight tremble in her hand as she reached out to direct the footmen. Frost could tell that Daisy had noticed it too as she suddenly narrowed her eyes at her friend with concern stamped across her dainty features.

It was also evident to Foster that Daisy didn't want anyone else to notice her friend's case of nerves, as she suddenly began chattering to all and sundry about absolutely nothing. It was a very strange occurrence.

He had never known her to be so well able to talk for so long about nothing. It was rather endearing until Amelia started to laugh.

"Enough, Daisy, I'm fine," Amelia finally whispered to her friend.

Foster nearly flinched at the warmth contained in the smile Daisy offered his sister-in-law. He didn't want to be jealous of his brother's wife. But why couldn't Daisy look at him with even a degree of that warmth?

Thankfully the new cook at Everleigh was highly skilled and the servants were very well trained. The evening passed without too much discomfort on anyone's part. Frost comforted himself that if worse came to worst that week, he could just concentrate on the meals Amelia would have served and all would be fine even if the company was doltish.

But it was unlikely his new sisters would have invited anyone that dreadful if they were really trying to match their friend into a good marriage. It was likely he was already acquainted with whomever they had invited. He hadn't bothered to inquire. But he expected most of the guests would be from the surrounding counties, as he was sure the young women would hope to live close to one another. Even Gilbert and Caroline didn't live terribly far from Everleigh in an estate that Caroline's father had handed over to them upon their marriage.

At least any of the male guests, that was. Foster couldn't even begin to hazard a guess as to who they might have invited to even out their numbers. He also wondered if any of Daisy's brothers would turn up. Reed had insisted that he had no interest but there were still her oldest and youngest brothers who would have likely been given an invitation.

He supposed he would know for certain the next day.

Foster felt like more of an observer than a participant as the evening unfolded. It reminded him of when he had first seen Daisy after so many years at the ball where he'd also encountered her brother, Reed. He only hoped he and Daisy would be able to be more civil than they had been that evening. He also wondered whether or not Simmons was going to be a fellow guest. His mind drifted back to that evening.

Foster knew he was being daft for showing concern over Daisy Alcott when he tried to convince her brother that they ought to remain by Daisy's side. She had been defending herself quite handily for years even though he was of the opinion that as the youngest of six children she ought to have at least five avid defenders just as he and his brothers stood up for their youngest brother. Not that Daisy was anything like his baby brother. Besides Daisy wouldn't allow such action on her behalf, he knew. She had been tearing a strip off him for his troubles for years.

Proverbially, of course. On the surface, the girl was as sweet as they come. She hid her vicious streak quite well from most. Her siblings were probably well aware. And he had made the mistake of getting on her bad side years ago and had never been able to right the wrong.

For some reason that rankled. And so, through the years, until he left home, he found himself always needling her in order to get a reaction. He supposed in the deep recesses of his mind he must have figured he would take any attention from her, even if it was the negative sort. But he could manage to keep himself away from the pretty young woman. Or rather he should manage it. It didn't seem as though he were doing a terribly good job of staying away from her at the moment.

Not that she was so very young anymore. That wasn't to say that she was a crone, either. But having lost an uncle and a couple of grandparents in recent years, Daisy had missed a few Seasons after her first was cut short. Now she was older than most of the debutantes gracing the Season, and Foster was sure it made the girl uncomfortable.

Somehow, he was torn between wanting to fix it for her and wanting to gloat over it.

And still he didn't think it was right that she be left to her own devices. She was far from a Society matron. Surely, she ought to be chaperoned at the very least.

But he wasn't her family nor was he really even her friend, so he ought not be concerning himself in the least. With a slight shake of his head and a stifled sigh but without another word, Frost followed Reed Alcott away from his sister's side.

"Don't know what you were doing hanging about her. Daisy has never tolerated you well. At least not since the incident."

Foster forced a chuckle, not having any desire to think about that terrible experience. He needed to keep his mind off Daisy Alcott and any other distractions he might be facing. He had more pressing matters to attend to. And then he needed to get back to his own affairs. Ladies seeking marriage were not for him. He needed to amass a greater fortune than Ash before he would consider settling down. And since Ashford had a four-year jump on him despite being the younger brother, Frost had some catching up to do.

Of course, he had sufficient confidence in his abilities that he expected to close the gap in no more than another twelve months, but still, distractions wouldn't help his efforts in the least.

He had only returned to England out of a mawkish wish to meet his two new sisters.

Frost and his brothers had always wished for sisters. Of course, they had wanted the sort that came in pigtails and short skirts that they could watch grow up, but he would make do with the two he had and hope for nieces he could watch over one day. He couldn't even bear to consider possible daughters of his own. That would be the biggest distraction ever and would deplete his slowly amassing fortune for certain. One day, though, he promised himself as he carried on with his old friend.

It was a challenge to listen to Reed blather on about the various amusements he was enjoying. Being the much-indulged middle son of a boisterous, loving family, Reed didn't seem to share any of the same interests that Foster now did. But their shared childhood ensured they were still fast friends despite their divergent present circumstances.

"Your sister-in-law invited me to a party at Everleigh," he was saying. "I hope she won't be terribly offended when I cry off. But surely, she can't expect me to attend."

Foster had to laugh. "I rather think that's why she sent you an invitation, my good man."

"Well, that was daft of her. She does have a brother, so she ought to know better."

"Attending a house party doesn't guarantee you'll have to wed, Reed," Foster answered, unable to keep the dry note out of his voice.

"It might not guarantee it, but it's near enough. Just look at Gilbert."

"Gil seems quite content with the outcome of his one foray into house parties."

"But see, all it took was one."

Foster shook his head having no interest in pursuing this particular conversation. "Then send your regrets. Amelia doesn't strike me as the sort to hold a grudge."

They settled down at a table that had been set up in the library for cards. A quick glance around showed Frost that he and Reed were the youngest gentlemen in the room. It amused him to no end. "You ought to come with me when I return to America if you're that dead set against marriage."

Reed wrinkled his nose at the suggestion. "Sounds a little too much like work if you ask me."

Foster laughed. "Your aunt should never have left you an inheritance. You are the laziest creature I've ever met."

Reed shrugged. "I'm sure you've met worse; you just didn't know it. I can assure you that I am not the superlative of anything."

Frost shook his head. Perhaps Reed was right. He might not be the most of anything, but he was a good sport and good company, and Foster was determined to enjoy his company despite their disparate views of life these days. And it certainly wasn't Reed's fault that Foster felt an inborn competition with his brothers.

Pushing all unwelcome thoughts away for a time, Frost enjoyed a few rounds of cards with his friend before he excused himself from the male-only company in their host's library. Foster knew, even though she was long dead, his mother would consider it the height of rudeness to be invited to a ball and not do at least a little bit of dancing.

With a frown, he realized that Daisy was not partnered, nor did she seem to have moved far from where he and Reed had left her. Was the girl not being invited to dance? That seemed highly unlikely. Perhaps he had just arrived at a fortuitous time. While Daisy might hate him, she wouldn't be able to decline his invitation, he was sure.

"Could I trouble you to partner me in the next minuet?"

She was obviously not expecting him. To his surprise, the girl he always thought had the steadiest nerves of anyone in his acquaintance nearly jumped from her skin at his question.

Clutching her chest overdramatically, the chit scolded him. "Foster Northcott, you should never sneak up on a lady like that. If I had shrieked from my surprise, you can only imagine the scandal that would erupt."

"You are being ridiculous, Daisy. Quite unforgivably so, in my estimation. For one thing, what are you doing being startled in a large, crowded room like this? Seems to me you must have been wool-gathering when you ought to be paying attention to the matter at hand."

Amusement filled him as the girl opened her mouth to argue with him but then shut it swiftly. He could see the moment when she realized she could not fault his reasoning. Suddenly, her face transformed from anger to awkwardness before him.

"My apologies, Mr. Northcott, I suppose," she returned grudgingly. "I am uncertain if there will be another minuet this evening."

"Well then, dance with me whatever the next one is. I'm sure you know them all."

His concluding statement chased away her awkwardness and she offered him a tight smile. "I have been taught well."

It was a half answer. From it, he surmised that she hadn't been getting as much practice as she would have liked. A frown gathered on his forehead even as he drew her hand into his elbow to escort her onto the dance floor.

"Never say an Alcott has been a wallflower."

"Very well, I shan't say it," she returned swiftly making, Frost's frown deepen.

"How is this possible?"

Daisy shrugged. "I didn't quite take the first time I came up for the Season. That one was cut short due to Grandmama's death. Then I didn't come up for two more years. Now I think people are of the opinion there's some hidden reason why I never wed."

Something in the area Frost suspected housed his heart pinched a little at the way the young woman in his arms tried to dismiss the matter, as though she cared very little one way or the other. But he knew that couldn't possibly be the case. For one thing, the Daisy Alcott he remembered was remarkably competitive. He was certain she would see this as a failure on her part. And she would chafe at it.

Foster also knew Daisy was friends with his two new sisters-in-law. It probably rankled that they had wed long before she did. And even her sisters were getting on with their lives. Frost knew how it felt to be left behind. Despite their history of rancor, his heart went out to the woman. It couldn't be easy. And yet she wasn't wringing her hands expecting people to feel sorry for her. In fact, she had sent him and her brother away so that she could see to the matter on her own. That was just like the Daisy he remembered.

Well, perhaps not the only Daisy he remembered. He remembered how trusting and confiding she had once been, before the incident. It was true that as the youngest child in a family of six, she had been markedly independent, trying to do the same as all her siblings. But she had still held a childish note he had found endearing as a boy. Probably because he didn't have any sisters, he tried to assure himself. It couldn't possibly be that he had developed feelings for the girl when they had been just children.

"What about Lord Simmons?"

"I beg your pardon?" The sudden turn of subject had clearly taken her by surprise, if the height of her eyebrows and the opening of her mouth were any indication.

"You are in Town to find yourself a husband, are you not? He would probably make you a good one." Foster didn't want to think about the pit that formed in his stomach at the thought of his friend's young sister

married to someone. *But Lord Simmons was a good fellow, a man you could count on, with a prosperous estate. He had also never been a rake and was only just now beginning to look for a viscountess after having settled into his inheritance for a couple of years. He also didn't have a mother who would meddle in his affairs as she had remarried, his sisters were already married off, and his brothers were off at Eton. For a moment, Frost quite hated him.*

"Have you run mad during your time at sea crossing back and forth between here and the uncivilized colonies?"

"They aren't so very uncivilized, Daisy. You ought to see them for yourself."

"Before or after I wed with Lord Simmons?"

The sarcasm dripping from her lips made Foster grin. "Perhaps before. No after. It wouldn't do for you to show up there unattached. There would be a queue a mile long for your hand, and there would be no way for you to make a sensible choice."

She didn't have a rejoinder for that and suddenly, Frost wondered if she were right. Perhaps he had gone daft. She wasn't wrong to suspect it.

"Come along, that's our number," *Foster declared, even though it was clearly not a minuet that the small orchestra was striking up.*

Instead of arguing, Daisy laughed and took his hand, following him in the familiar steps. Foster's heart tripped over itself. He wouldn't mind getting used to the sensation of Daisy Alcott willingly following him into anything.

But he had other things to take care of besides a fortune to amass. And Daisy hated him anyway. She loved to dance so she hadn't refused him, but he wasn't so daft as to think that constituted her forgiveness.

"Why Simmons?" She demanded in between one of the sets, and Frost had to search his mind in question of what she was talking about. The delight spreading across her face told him she knew she had confounded him.

"He's nice, wealthy, and unencumbered."

Her left eyebrow quirked at him in question but then she turned her gaze to the side of the ballroom where the gentleman in question could be seen in conversation with a small group of known political associates.

"Is he active in the House?"

"That I'm not certain of, but as a Lord, I would expect so."

Foster's stomach clenched at the assessing expression upon Daisy's face. He was the one who had started it; he had no one to blame but himself.

"Perhaps I will check if Amelia has invited him to her party," he heard himself say and wished to cut out his own tongue.

"Why are you trying your hand at matchmaking, Frost? Are you that bored to be home?"

"I'm not really home. Not yet anyway."

"What is that supposed to mean?"

Foster was relieved when the steps separated them again, and he hoped she would drop the subject.

"You aren't going to stay, are you?" She said it almost as an accusation, but there was little heat in it. Foster was relieved that Daisy didn't expect to have a hand in controlling him. His new sisters were doing enough of that for all of England.

And Frost had too many matters to take care of to indulge any of his relations, let alone the newest ones. And certainly not his old friend or enemy, whichever category Daisy Alcott fell into.

"As I said, not yet."

"What do you have against England?"

She didn't seem to be accusatory, merely curious.

"I have absolutely nothing against it. I love our country and king and all of that. But I have to do something with myself, Daisy. Surely you understand that. Not everyone can have an aunt pass and leave them an estate like Reed has."

Her face softened in that way she had, and Foster almost lost his mind and revealed all his secrets in that moment.

"I'm pleased for Reed but worry about Laurence for that. Aunt Gertrude left him a little but not the windfall that Reed got." She sighed and looked away. "I know. We all face our challenges." When she turned back to him, there was an urgency about her he hadn't seen before. "You will be careful, though, won't you?"

Foster grinned. "Always. Lucian has threatened to reach beyond the grave and beat me if I don't always come home alive."

That had the intended result, making Daisy's face lighten and laughter spill between them. But then Foster dampened it again.

"Amelia is counting on you to make up her numbers, Daisy. Don't leave her waiting on you."

Foster's frown matched hers. She was clearly puzzled over his insistence. And he couldn't explain it either. He didn't have time for complications at this juncture. He was being ridiculous to be stirring up trouble for himself in the shape of one beautiful young woman. There was no time for him to cajole forgiveness from her. And he couldn't complicate his situation with a wife just yet. There was his fortune to think about, and then there were those other matters. The ones his brother Gilbert needed him to look into.

"Tell me what you thought of Amelia when first you made her acquaintance."

"I'll tell you after you've promised to turn up at her party."

Daisy's brow wrinkled in a charming fashion. "I had intended to accept, Frost, but your insistence is making me nervous. What aren't you telling me?"

Foster stifled a curse. He was truly being beyond daft this night. "There is naught I'm not telling you; I swear it. I am merely anxious to please my new sister."

Her assessing gaze made sweat prickle between his shoulder blades. She had always been a keen observer; it unnerved him to wonder what she could see.

Foster blinked, coming back to the present, only to encounter Daisy's assessing gaze upon him once again. He turned to Caroline and engaged her in conversation.

***

The day dawned bright and clear. Frost had finally slept soundly after having now been off the boat for over a week. It was the strangest thing that the land sickness lasted with him longer than ever seasickness did. He was up with the sun and out on one of his father's many horses, the pounding hooves sounding loud and wonderful in his ears. There was something about riding neck and nothing over the heath that could not compare to anything he had ever found in the new world.

He supposed it was where one's roots were grown that influenced the type of things one loved the most. It was for that reason that he knew he would return to England to live his life when he felt that he had finally reached the level of success required to be satisfied. It was also why he was searching for money-making investments closer to home now that he had enough money to seed some ventures here. He had a suspicion that he would never be satisfied now that he knew what it was to make money of his own.

Having heard the stories from Caroline and Gilbert about how her father wasn't well received due to his money being in factories, Frost was torn between defying those naysayers and ensuring he didn't invest in anything that would be considered bourgeois. He knew that as the Earl of Everleigh's son, it was unlikely that he would ever be given the cut like Mr. Smith had been. But he did have a future wife to consider.

And why did an image of Daisy Alcott conjure itself in his mind at that thought? She was not for him. Never mind that she hated him, she also wanted to wed soon, and he could not find it in himself to settle down at this stage.

He urged his horse to a faster pace, hoping to outrun his restless thoughts. After an hour of hard riding, he found himself rubbing down the horse, whispering soothing sounds to the sweating creature.

"Rode her hard, you did, sir," the groom commented, his tone expressing both admiration and admonition.

"She's a good girl with plenty of bottom, isn't she?" Frost knew to compliment the stable staff if he wanted them to let him have another creature in the future.

The rugged ride had settled him, and Foster was more than ready to break his fast. As luck would have it, the first person he encountered was Daisy, filling her plate from the sideboard.

"Good morning," she greeted him with a sunny smile.

Evidently, she was the type of person who loves the morning, he realized with a slight grumble as he returned her smile and greeting with something akin to a grunt. Having brothers apparently made the girl immune to taking offense at his churlish morning attitude. Even though he had chosen to rise with the sun and had enjoyed the rousing ride, he wasn't prepared to entertain conversation until he had been fortified with some food and coffee. He thought there might have been a quickly suppressed giggle coming from her direction, but Frost couldn't be bothered to check. After everything they had coldly said to one another in the recent past, Foster wasn't prepared to be terribly warm with Daisy Alcott. He didn't care what his sleep-deprived heart might think on the matter.

His rough accommodations in Canada were no place for a gently bred young woman, and he didn't intend to set up another establishment for some time yet. So, no matter what his charming new sisters thought, he was not going to be matched during their house party. Perhaps he ought to have breakfast brought to his room like a lady for the rest of the week. That thought brought him out of his doldrums. Well, that, and the heaping plate of food that he was already tucking into.

Daisy was at the other end of the table quietly chatting with Foster's youngest brother about his studies when Foster finally brought himself to care about his surroundings more than his plate.

Foster's youngest brother was blissfully unconcerned about his lot in life. It was a state that Frost couldn't comprehend. Somehow it was an idea planted in his head from what he suspected was the moment his next brother, Ashford, had been born. The urge to compete for attention, for his place, for the feeling of success. Foster rather thought the competitive feelings had been more directed toward his two older brothers when he was young. He could recall trying to outdo them in all endeavours. And if any teacher had ever compared them in school, Frost could well remember the hot sensation that had flooded him, making his palms sweat and his scalp tingle.

But then one of their father's old friends had invited Ash to go to sea with him, taking his younger brother out of school and setting him up as his apprentice of sorts. And Ashford had started to amass his fortune. It was quite unheard of for the fourth son. But obviously not impossible. Upon reading the first letter from Ash in which money was mentioned, it was then and there that Foster's competitive nature had taken over, and he had felt forced by his own temperament to ensure that he succeeded even more than his younger brother.

The fact that Ashford had more help and more time didn't seem to alter Foster's convictions. And so here he was, sitting in his childhood home, by choice, he reminded himself, but still anxious to get back to the colonies and his many businesses and interests there. He knew they wouldn't fall apart without him. But he also knew they wouldn't grow or advance without him there to oversee everything. So, he needed to get this visit out of the way, help his brother with the little matter that had brought him home at this particular time, and then get back on a ship before the seasons turned and a crossing would be inadvisable. Foster had no intention of cooling his heels in England for six months or more, waiting out the winter. He would cross as soon as he was able. But he would also cross in the winter if need be. It wouldn't actually much alter the discomfort of the crossing, merely making it colder than usual. Possibly more dangerous if the boat were to ice, but the salt should prevent that.

It mattered little. He wouldn't dally. They were early enough; he should be able to finish things here and be gone well before he need worry.

"Are you still getting used to being awake, Foster? I would have thought after a ride and a full meal you'd be restored by now." Daisy's gentle question brought Foster's attention back into the breakfast room.

Foster grinned at her way of putting it.

"I'm well used to being awake, but that doesn't necessarily mean I'm happy about that state."

A light tinkle of laughter followed his statement, and Foster felt his chest well with pride that he had amused her. And then he dismissed himself for being ridiculous.

"So where did you go?" Daisy asked with her head tilted to one side, looking very much like an inquisitive little animal.

"For my ride?" Foster asked. "I rode along the heath, revisiting many of my old haunts from boyhood."

"That must have been lovely," she murmured. "But actually, I meant right now, in your mind. It was evident that you had disappeared and were no longer with us in the breakfast room."

Foster laughed again at her turn of phrase. "I can assure you that I was right here the entire time."

She made a humming noise as though she didn't believe him and was in fact annoyed that he would tell her a tale. But Foster wasn't about to tell her what he had really been doing out on the moors nor what had been on his mind when he had 'left the room' as she said.

"Frost has always had the ability to be here and gone at the same time," Roderick commented to Daisy with a laugh. "It is an ability he particularly enjoys when I start talking to him about my latest studies."

"That was exceptional, Roddy, and well you know it. I was exhausted, and you wanted to talk about some sort of beetle you were examining. It failed to stimulate my exhausted mind, I'm afraid."

Roderick and Daisy both laughed.

"What would it have taken to keep your attention, then, Foster? What is it that has drawn you so inexorably to the colonies? Do you enjoy the wilds so very much?"

Daisy's questions made Foster join in the laughter. "There are many places that are no longer so wild. You would be surprised at how advanced things are there.

In some ways far more advanced than here, as they are not mired in hundreds of years of tradition."

"Isn't everyone over there from over here? I would think the traditions would be quite similar."

Frost nodded to acknowledge the truth of her words but then added his own observation. "The only difference being that everyone who has made their way to the colonies has been searching for a fresh start of some sort. So, they aren't nearly as mired in history as we are. And when you start and build fresh, without all the old things as a foundation, it progresses in varied directions."

Daisy stared at him with wonder in her eyes. "You love it there, don't you?" Her statement was almost accusatory, as though she couldn't imagine anyone loving anywhere other than their little corner of Kent.

Foster shrugged. "It's a challenge to love both places nearly equally. They are so very different from one another. And both with their beauty. But here is far more clean than there. And already developed, besides. I do love the wilds, though, you are correct in that. I do hope you get to see it for yourself one day."

"I am not certain I could bear the crossing. What's the best time you've ever made?"

"Six weeks," Foster declared, what sounded like awe in his tone. "It usually only takes about six weeks now. Not that I have actually crossed so very many times. This is only my third time home since I left."

"What's the worst crossing?"

"Of my six crossings, the second was the worst. It only took a couple extra days, but they were rough days. It used to take far longer, though, when the captains didn't know what to expect and the boats weren't as robust for the seas they might encounter."

"But what do you do for six weeks? I would think the boredom would be the worst part of it."

"There is no shortage of work to be done onboard, but perhaps not for a lady."

Foster bit back a smile as Daisy appeared offended by his words. "I do not consider work to be beneath me."

"Perhaps not, but it might not be the safest place for you."

She opened her mouth as though to argue with him and then shut it abruptly, making Foster struggle to hide his amusement. She had only changed in that she was better able to prevent the harsh words that sprang to her mind, but she was still as easy to bait as ever. It would be diverting to use that ability in the coming week.

But then he thought better of it. The chit was trying to arrange her life. He could well relate to the sentiment. That was why he was so determined to return to Upper Canada. He had unfinished business to take care of there. He had no desire to put a spoke in her wheels. She deserved the future she was hoping for.

It was with relief that he observed the arrival of his hostess and new sister-in-law.

Chapter Five

"Good morning," Amelia called out in an overly cheerful tone, causing Daisy to wonder what her friend was thinking.

"I was wondering where you were," Daisy commented.

"Would you believe, increasing is shockingly tiring? I was quite glued to my bedding this morning. Have you been well served?"

"Of course," Daisy answered promptly, with a smile. "It would seem you run an efficient household here, Ames." Her friend grinned over her use of the old nickname. "Was it challenging to take over the running of the house?"

"Not in the least," Amelia answered immediately. "I think his lordship was just waiting for someone to do it."

Daisy was surprised when both Roderick and Foster chuckled over Amelia's words. "You might very well be correct, my lady," Foster acknowledged with a nod. "And it's a good thing Lucian didn't keep him waiting any longer, or the house might have fallen down around us."

"I don't suppose Lucian has much to do with it," Amelia replied with a tart tone, making Daisy hide her amusement and Foster start to sputter.

"Well, he married you, didn't he?"

"That was the most sensible thing, wasn't it?"

"Absolutely, and look what it brought us, a woman to save us all."

Daisy held her breath while her friend decided how she was going to react to her brother-in-law's goading. She was relieved when Amelia chose to ignore the irritation. Their hostess' smile was a little strained but at least it was pinned in place as she turned toward Daisy.

"I've been meaning to ask you, how well acquainted are you with Lady Constance? I know she was friendly with my sister when Ellen made her debut, but that was even before we made ours."

Daisy was forced to stifle her amusement. Amelia's tone implied that Constance was nearly a crone. It didn't help Daisy with her feelings of growing old and missing her chance at matrimony. But at least she wasn't as old as Constance was, from what she inferred from Amelia's words. It set her teeth on edge, but she tried not to overreact. Obviously, her friend meant no offence.

"We've met, but I don't know her terribly well. I do know she has chosen to travel with a companion after one of her relations left her an inheritance. It caused a bit of a stir that verged on the scandalous."

Amelia's eyes glowed with excitement at the thought of a juicy tidbit, but she was quick to wave her hand as though to dismiss the thought. "There is surely nothing scandalous in a woman seeing a little more of the world."

"Of course, there isn't. But some like to see scandal in every possible corner. I only wish I had a long-lost relation who wished to leave me a bequest so I could follow in her ladyship's wake."

"Truly?" Amelia sounded scandalized.

Daisy laughed and then sighed. "No, not truly. I am sufficiently conventional that I would wish to wed before travelling the world. Or at least travelling a little bit. I'm not completely certain I would be cut out for crossing the Atlantic. But I've always wished to see some other places like France or Belgium."

"Why not an ocean crossing?" Foster interjected himself into their conversation. Out of nowhere anger swept through Daisy.

"Need you ask how I feel about water?" Her tone was unpleasant, but she was too full of outrage to care. *Did he even need to ask?* She tried to hold her breath along with her equilibrium, but it was a close run thing, especially when she saw irritation cloud Foster's gaze.

"Surely you've overcome that long ago grievance."

Daisy ignored his statement, turning her attention back to Amelia.

"Why did you ask if I know Constance?"

"I've just received word that she is on the way here. I had sent her an invitation, but it would seem it took a long time to reach her, and I'm just now receiving her reply. It will upset my numbers a trifle, but that can be easily remedied. Perhaps I can prevail upon your brother to come after all."

Daisy forced a laugh even as she was curious. "Which one?"

"I was hoping for Reed, but he insisted he was busy. I think he just couldn't be bothered. But just now I was thinking of Florent. He is nearby. He wouldn't even have to come and stay over if he doesn't want to, but he could even out my numbers when we want to be formal."

"Has he already declined?" Daisy was curious. Since it was true that he resided nearby, she wondered if he had not yet received an invitation.

"We spoke of it previously, but he thought he might be too busy."

Daisy wasn't sure why her friend was asking about her brother. It seemed to her as though there might be some sort of context to the inquiry, but she was too distracted by Foster's departure from the room to ask any further questions at that moment. He seemed put out by her irritation with him. A very momentary impulse to run after him swept through her. With a shake of her head, Daisy admonished herself not to be beyond foolish.

As the day progressed, more guests arrived, which kept everyone busy. Daisy was surprised that Lord Merton was the first to arrive in the early afternoon. She had thought, after his comments about the roads in his neighbourhood, that he would take a long time to make the journey to Everleigh. But it turned out maybe he wasn't nearly as persnickety as he had let on. Daisy was also surprised by her reaction when she witnessed his arrival. His blond hair and blue eyes, which she had considered insipid in the ballroom, were actually highly attractive as viewed in the sunshine in the forecourt of Everleigh House.

When Lord Simmons arrived, Daisy found herself looking for Foster, as he had been the one to recommend Lord Simmons as a potential for Daisy to consider. But Foster was nowhere to be seen. It was most odd. Daisy found herself distracted throughout the day, looking for Foster, which angered her to no end. Angry with herself. It wasn't his fault she was being a dolt. She didn't even like the man! Why was she looking for him? And yet she found herself wondering what he would think of the moment, the new arrival, or whatever had been said. She wished for his opinion or wondered if he would be amused as she was by each passing fancy. It was most disheartening and even infuriating now with the arrival of Lords Merton and Simmons. Daisy ought to be preoccupied with those two gentlemen – the most eligible men Amelia could have invited to her house party. And yet Daisy would continue to be distracted by thoughts of Foster and where he might have gone off to.

The other gentlemen's arrival reminded Daisy of her conversation with Foster at the last ball she attended before coming to Everleigh. Her mind drifted back to that evening. It had been surprising and odd how very much advice Foster wanted to give her. She wondered if he would be offering her any more that week.

Daisy's examination of Foster Northcott answered very few of the questions traipsing through her mind. But the one thing that stood out for her in that moment was that despite their convoluted history, she felt safe in his arms. She put it down to familiarity but nearly tripped in the steps when the thought crossed her mind. She couldn't feel safe in Frost's arms! She didn't trust him. If he couldn't be counted on to save a bag of kittens or a drowning girl, she couldn't count on him for anything beyond the steps of this dance.

She kept a polite smile pinned to her face as she averted her gaze from his. She was pleased to see that they were attracting attention. Perhaps that would spur another gentleman into asking her to dance. Daisy couldn't bear to face another Season without a match. Would she have to remain a spinster?

Daisy knew she was hardly a spinster yet and ought not think of herself in this vein, but it was hard not to do so when she was so eager and ready to move on to the next stages of her life. It felt to her as though she were just putting in time, waiting for her future to arrive. She didn't want to wait any longer.

It was hard to fathom, but perhaps dancing with Foster was going to trigger that arrival. Strange things happened every day. This could be one of them.

Daisy wasn't such a fool that she would refuse a gift, no matter its source. She fortified the smile she knew had been slipping from her face. It wouldn't benefit her to appear to be grimacing even if that might be her impulse under the circumstances.

Ought she to make eye contact with the various gentlemen watching? Would that attract their attention or paint her as overly bold? Why was this so hard? Why couldn't it be like in the books she enjoyed from the circulating library? Further reflection reminded her that those tales usually resulted in a love match and that wasn't what she was after. So it should, in theory, actually be easier for her. Those stories often had twists and turns and complications on their way to happily ever after. Since she wanted a very straight forward arrangement with a suitable husband in which they lived their independent lives, she didn't see why it had to be quite so difficult.

Her sigh must not have been as quiet as she had thought. Foster's fingers tightened where they were clasping hers in the dance, reminding her that she had allowed her thoughts to wander. It was most unusual. How could she hate the man and yet feel so comfortable in his company? Again, she attributed it to the long acquaintance she and her family had with Foster and his brothers.

"I think you are putting too much effort into it, Daisy. I know you have always had the independent urge and you want to do it all yourself. I completely understand that, as I have it myself. That's probably why I recognize it so clearly in you. But I think, in this one case, you have to let it come to you."

Daisy blew an errant strand of hair out of her eye in an effort to release the pent-up frustrations threatening to overwhelm her.

"What does that even mean, Foster? This is my life or my future life under discussion. How could you possibly think I would just stand by and let it happen on its own?"

"I don't mean that it will miraculously happen on its own. I mean that you cannot force it. That you have to *allow the gentleman to pick you. It shouldn't take long, nor should it be difficult. You are a lovely, articulate young woman of good family. I'm certain your dowry is respectable. You are undoubtedly well educated in all the things young ladies ought to be educated in. It shouldn't be long before there is a queue of gentlemen just waiting to claim you as the mistress of their homes."*

For the briefest moment joy burst into her heart and Daisy had to catch her breath over it.

"That's quite the loveliest thing anyone has ever said to me, Frost, and I'm quite stunned that it came out of you, to be perfectly frank. But why hasn't it happened yet? This is the third week of the Season already. And there is no queue of which you spoke."

"Because you've been trying to force it." Foster's seemingly patient tone set Daisy's teeth on edge, but she managed to keep her irritation under rein. "Gentlemen are like stubborn, unbroken horses. You need to let them come to you or you'll never have them eating out of your hand."

Blinking, Daisy stared at him even as she followed his lead through the next turns in the dance. "Why in the name of heaven would I want them to eat from my hand?"

Now it was his turn to stare at her. "I didn't mean literally!"

Daisy nearly missed her next step as heat filled her chest and her cheeks flamed. If only the wooden floor beneath their feet could open up and swallow her entirely. She opened her mouth to excuse her ignorance, but no words would come out.

Foster's rich laughter sounded, thankfully muted so as not to draw too much attention, but it both deepened her embarrassment and somehow assuaged it as well. Daisy returned his grin.

"I knew that," she said sheepishly, *willing the glow to recede from her cheeks.*

"Did you, though?" he asked with a teasing glint in his eyes.

Daisy controlled her urge to swat him on the shoulder like the bug that he was and concentrated on the steps of the dance as well as the topic they were discussing rather than the manner in which it was delivered.

"I suppose I ought to have known that with three brothers," she finally muttered in a sheepish manner, unable to meet his knowing gaze.

Foster smiled and nodded. *"Perhaps, but I suppose husbands are a rather different topic than brothers, so your forgetfulness on the matter could be excused."*

"But how could you have known or thought about this? And why would you go to the bother of helping me?"

Foster lifted his shoulder as though it weren't a matter of importance and for a moment Daisy thought he wasn't going to answer her. Finally, he looked her in the eye and made the bottom drop out of her stomach. *"I suppose I owed you one."*

Blessedly their dance, which had begun to seem interminable, came to an end before Daisy had to offer up a reply. She managed to avoid the entire uncomfortable encounter by curtsying her thanks for the dance and turning from him.

"See you at Everleigh," he called after her in a controlled voice that didn't carry too far but still caused a few heads to turn their way. Daisy kept her stride and pace in check and willed her cheeks to remain cool. She reached the refreshment table without anyone else intervening, much to her intense relief.

A few sips of the tepid punch had her usual equilibrium restored.

It *didn't* matter what Foster said or thought, she reminded herself fiercely. He was nobody to her.

Men are not horses to eat out of my hand, she also iterated, rather needlessly in her opinion. Of course, he was speaking metaphorically. She just wasn't used to him being intelligent or wise.

But sadly, he did have a point. Standing on the side of the dance floor willing appropriate gentlemen to approach her had not been the least bit successful and was no doubt twisting her face into an unapproachable mask. She would have to come up with a new strategy.

"Miss Alcott?"

Daisy was proud of herself that she had managed not to startle and spill the punch down the front of her gown. She really needed to stop wool gathering in a crowded room. It was ridiculous to be surprised to hear herself addressed. She turned with a smile to see who was addressing her.

And quickly curtsied.

"My lord, how do you do?"

It was Viscount Merton, a pleasant, reputedly wealthy, highly eligible peer who was rumored to finally be seeking a match. He was also the heir to the Marquis of Airdrie. Daisy hadn't ever set her sights that high. She wasn't certain if she wanted her sights set that high.

But the man wasn't proposing. He had merely said her name. Or actually asked it? She was wool gathering again. She tried not to sigh as she offered him what she hoped was a winning smile, grateful for once that her thoughts raced enough that no time had passed.

"This is to be the supper dance. Could I partner you?"

How the time had flown! The supper dance. With Viscount Merton. What a coup. And yet Daisy's inner delight was sorely lacking. She would take herself to task later. For now, she made the appropriate response *of putting her hand into his elbow and allowing him to escort her back toward the dance floor.*

How could Foster have been right? Dancing with him brought other gentlemen to heel? And now she was comparing them to dogs rather than horses. She was worse than Frost. She tried to turn her mind toward some sort of conversation with the gentleman but then remembered Frost's advice – let the men come to her. Well, he had come to her. But now she supposed she ought to let him continue taking the lead, not just in the dance steps but also in the conversation.

It did not sit well with her independent, take charge soul, but she did her best to curb that side of herself, at least for the moment.

"I was sorry to hear about your losses. You were missed in Town."

"That is so kind of you to say, my lord."

And unexpected. But Daisy kept that thought to herself.

"How did you keep yourself occupied while stuck at Alcott?"

Daisy wasn't sure exactly how to answer that question. Was this some sort of interview to ascertain if she had appropriate pastimes? Or was it merely a conversation between two acquaintances who knew very little about one another?

"There is much to keep one occupied on an estate such as my father's. And with my sisters gone from the house, there is only me and my mother to see to much of it. So, despite our sadness, we were very busy most of the time."

"Which occupations interest you the most?" He was persistent, that much she would give him. She supposed she could appreciate that quality as she had it herself.

"Visiting the tenants is probably my favorite as there is such variety in it. The gardening might be my second

favorite," she mused, never having really given thought to which activities were her favorite in order like that.

"Do you not have gardeners at Alcott House?"

Daisy laughed. "Of course, we do, but my mother, as I'm sure you realize from all our names, has always fancied being a botanist, so we've all been expected to take a hand in the gardens and pull our weight, as it were."

"Are you very good at it? And do you fancy yourself a botanist like your mother?"

Daisy laughed lightly again. "Not in the least. Well, I'm reasonably good at it in that I can keep plants alive and can usually tell the difference between a weed and a plant so as to not destroy the gardens. But I don't have the imagination for trying to create new plants or anything like that. I'm far too practical. My favorite flowers already exist and are in very artful arrangements in the gardens quite nicely without giving me any cause to think they ought to be arranged. And for the rest, I quite like the usual types of vegetables and fruit, so I don't have an intense urge to experiment as does my mother."

She paused for a moment before adding. "That isn't to say that an experiment or two might not be interesting. I can understand her interest in seeing if some things might grow in our climate even if they were from somewhere else. I don't think anyone minds having oranges when really they ought not exist here." She laughed and lifted her shoulder. "So, is that perhaps a maybe in answer to your question?"

To her relief the viscount laughed lightly along with her, and she was emboldened to ask him in return, "Do you have extensive gardens at Merton? And do you ever take a hand in their design or function?"

"We have, as you said, well arranged pleasure gardens that were already well established by some *relative. I quite enjoy them so see no need to change them aside from whatever is needed to replace or maintain what is already there. But no, I have not ever stuck my fingers in the soil at Merton. I wonder if that makes me a terrible steward of my estate."*

Daisy lifted her eyebrows at him. "It's not too late to give it a try."

He stared at her as though to ascertain if she were serious or not. When he noted the glint in her eyes, he grinned at her. "Perhaps you could show me one day."

She nearly lost her consciousness of where they were in the steps. She would have been mortified. But years of training and practice kept her stepping properly, and no toes were trod upon as she regained her inner balance as well.

"Perhaps," she finally replied. Her heart fluttered. Not out of excitement that Lord Merton was considering her, but rather out of anger that Frost had been right.

How could one gentleman's dancing with her suddenly make her seem appealing to others? Or was it really the fact that she had left the ballroom altogether? As Frost had said, make them look for her, not the other way around. Daisy didn't know if she could bear to marry a man who was such a sheep.

But if she wanted her independent life, perhaps a sheep was exactly what she was looking for. She smiled at the viscount and tried to think of something not-overbearing to say.

Daisy returned her attention back to the present, still wondering where Foster had gotten himself off to. She tried to remind herself that she hated him, but there was very little heat to the sensation. She was beginning to worry about him. It was afternoon when he finally returned to the house, dishevelled.

Curiosity consumed Daisy once more. Where had Foster been? Why was he dishevelled? Why was he out riding when guests were arriving? Had he lost all sense of propriety while living amongst the wilds of the colonies? Was he not curious about Constance and her companion who had just arrived with a great deal of fanfare? Clearly not, but Daisy was curious about Foster and his whereabouts. If he didn't cease being so odd, Daisy was going to have to investigate.

Daisy tried to tamp down her inquisitiveness; she was bound to hurt Amelia's feelings. It was evident her friend had gone to a great deal of effort on this, her first big entertainment. The fact that she had made Daisy her guest of honor was, well, an honor. Daisy was being a terrible friend and a dreadful guest by not being in alt over her friend's arrangements.

The arrival of Lord and Lady Bathurst and their daughter, Annabelle, concluded that day's arrivals, and Amelia escorted everyone through to the reception room in anticipation of what was left of the day's activities. It was now late in the afternoon, and the latest arrivals were in their rooms getting tidied for the evening meal, which had been held a bit later than country hours to accommodate those later arrivals. Daisy felt a bit sorry for the Bathurst family who had just arrived, and she was once again grateful that Amelia had asked her to arrive a day early so she hadn't been forced to be terribly sociable after a long day of travel.

Another curious thing that Daisy wondered about and debated asking Caroline about was the absence of Caroline's husband, Gilbert. Daisy would have thought Gilbert would be present for Amelia and Caroline's house party, but he was noticeably absent. She didn't know him well, having only met him a time or two during her first, abbreviated Season, but from Caroline's letters it sounded as though the two were very devoted to one another. Even if they weren't, it seemed as though etiquette would require his presence.

This, too, was a distraction for Daisy. So many things to think about and no answers to her many questions.

It turned out that Daisy's mother was old friends with Lady Bathurst. Daisy had never seen her mother quite so boisterous. It was amusing to witness her mum acting like one of the debutantes, giggling and gossiping with her old friend. Lady Alcott wasn't even bothered by the fact that her son hadn't yet answered Amelia about whether or not he would attend her party. Daisy considered it the height of rudeness and would have gone home to collect him herself if she weren't the supposed guest of honour at the house party. She couldn't just slip away unnoticed in the middle of the day.

Daisy's maid made such a fuss over her toilette for the evening even though Amelia had said it would be a casual affair as everyone had just arrived. More guests were to arrive on the morrow and Daisy could see Amelia had paid particular attention to select entertaining fellow guests. Still, Daisy could not quite concentrate on the task at hand. She had two highly eligible bachelors to choose from. Lords Merton and Simmons were making an effort to be convivial and yet Daisy kept wondering about Foster.

On the third day that Daisy was there, when again she realized that Foster had gone out riding very early in the morning even though she knew Amelia had a ride planned that day, Daisy resolved that she would follow him the next day. He was acting highly suspicious, and Daisy was determined to get to the bottom of it. She didn't care that she risked her reputation and her opportunities with Lords Merton and Simmons. She couldn't find it in herself to put aside her intense interest. Foster was acting as though he were up to something. Perhaps something nefarious. Daisy told herself she was protecting her friend, Amelia, who was hostess now at Everleigh, but she wasn't quite able to fool herself. Staring at her reflection in the looking glass hanging in the large, lovely room she had been given, Daisy knew she was heading for trouble.

She had read or overheard someone once say that love and hate were very closely related. She wondered if that were true. Daisy was fully convinced that she hated Foster Northcott. He had treated her abominably as a young girl, and now he was a greedy man obsessed with accumulating more wealth than his brother. She ought to reject any thought about him.

Besides the fact that she had no interest in loving anyone. Nor hating them for that matter. Daisy wanted a serene life in a Society marriage. Independence was what she sought. Not some strange obsession with another human.

Chapter Six

Foster felt as though there were eyes trained upon him. A hundred eyes, a thousand eyes, all the eyes in the Kingdom. It was a ridiculous thought but not one he could easily shake. The most piercing of eyes were Daisy's. And that thought wasn't ridiculous at all.

What a silly name she had been given. Daisies were sunny and playful looking flowers. And he supposed she was that at times. But there was an intensity about her that often belied that sunny disposition. Like when she was watching him.

He wasn't sure what she was looking for. Foster had done his best to cover his actions. There was nothing objectionable about his going riding early in the morning or for a walk late at night. Amelia hadn't seemed to notice his absences, so he was confident he wasn't violating some social convention, but Daisy had certainly noticed. And continued to watch him with her inscrutable gaze. It made a very small part of him consider confiding in her.

But even if they were friends, he couldn't tell her what he was up to, even though he was well aware that she was consumed with curiosity.

The distracting thoughts were buzzing around in his mind as he concealed himself between a boulder and a scruffy shrub. It wasn't the best hiding place for his large body, but it was the best he could do. And if he held still enough, they wouldn't notice him. But his restless thoughts were making his limbs twitchy.

Twitching could get him killed.

He wasn't used to this sort of situation. He was not an agent of the Crown. It was hard for him to believe or accept that his brother was. If Foster thought about it, he supposed Gilbert was suited to the position. But Foster didn't think he himself was cut out for it. He was only doing this at his brother's request.

There had been a rather cryptic letter waiting for him when his ship had finally docked on English shores. Foster had been hard pressed to decipher it. It would seem that Gilbert had remembered the code they had made up as boys, but Foster had long ago relegated it to childhood stories. With a few fits and starts, though, he had been able to figure out that Gilbert suspected smugglers were using Everleigh lands to ply their trades.

Foster didn't like it but didn't consider it to be such a terrible thing that his brother considered it. But still, Gilbert had asked so here he was surveying the beach under the weak light of the moon that was half covered by a haze of clouds, trying not to get himself killed for his efforts.

Gilbert had insisted that as an agent for the Home Office, he couldn't allow his ancestral home to be used for such purposes. Foster had wished to shrug over that part. After his time in the Canadas, he had more of a live-and-let-live attitude. But it was Gil's concern that government agents could accuse their father or brother of colluding with the smugglers that had prompted Foster to go along with his brother's edicts.

He might be out of touch with current affairs in England, but he was aware of the tightening restrictions and penalties on those who plied the smuggling trade.

Gilbert hadn't been certain if it was cotton or brandy or maybe both being transported through this cove. It really mattered little. Both could carry a death penalty. Being peers might protect them from death, but the King and his government had been so put out by the efforts to evade the tax on such items that he had threatened to remove peers from their properties if they were to turn a blind eye.

Gil suspected their father would do so out of spite for being told not to. Foster wouldn't put it past the cantankerous old man. Neither of them wished to test their hypothesis and so, Foster found himself huddling in the uncomfortable position pushing thoughts of one watchful young woman from his mind, hoping to keep them all alive.

Including the smugglers, if there even were any.

Gilbert's letter hadn't gone into details about why he suspected there even were smugglers in this particular part of the country. It would certainly be out of the way and not the usual location. But perhaps that was the point. While Foster thought it was daft to ply a trade that could have you hung, it didn't mean smugglers were actually stupid. And still, Foster huddled in the cool autumn night, torn between hoping no one showed up and wishing they would so it would be over.

But that was a gullible way to think. There either were smugglers using Everleigh or there weren't. If there were, Foster would have to put an end to it and find out who at Everleigh had known. Neither Gilbert nor Foster wanted to involve their oldest brother, Viscount Adelaide. As a peer, Lucian was at risk of the consequences as much as their father.

Foster also suspected Lucian might be involved in the Home Office as well, though neither he nor Gilbert had said so. Frost shook his head. How did either of his brothers end up as government agents? It was the most confounding thing he could imagine. And not for him. He much preferred straightforward actions. None of this skulking about as Gilbert had him doing.

And needing to dodge Amelia's guests, especially Daisy, as he tried to figure out what was going on was sure to send him into an early grave if he couldn't keep his mind focused on the task at hand. If he wasn't mistaken, he could hear oars in the surf. It was obvious they were trying to be quiet. No one else in the vicinity would have noticed the sound, but he was straining his ears for any evidence to support his brother's claim.

He just wished that he hadn't.

Smugglers at Everleigh. Foster sighed. It had seemed like a lark. Almost like when they were children playing games. But this was no game. Lives were at stake on both sides of the issue.

Foster's life in Upper Canada skirted all sorts of things that English law might consider questionable. But even he paid his taxes when called upon. Especially if it was cotton they were smuggling; they were stealing from his friends. Hugh, Viscount of Richmond, was setting up his estate to produce even more wool and cotton this year than last. Bringing cotton into the country illegally would make things harder for Hugh and his tenant farmers.

England's recent love affair with velvet seemed to have made cotton the hottest commodity, and the government was determined to protect the locally grown industry, increasing the taxes on cotton from America and India, and causing those who wished to bring it into the country to skirt the customs officers. Foster would have wanted to ignore the issue if it weren't for the possibility of his ancestral home being used for such a lily-livered effort. Not to say that smugglers were cowards. Much the contrary, in Foster's opinion. But they were putting so many others at risk and for that reason, Foster couldn't very well stand by and do nothing.

But what was he supposed to do?

Foster fought unwelcome laughter. He had been so certain that Everleigh would be immune to such a situation as they weren't on the southern shores of the country. But he could see that Gilbert was right. The cove they were in was perfect. Being up the river a bit but not too far from the mouth to be able to row there easily made it far safer for the smugglers. And the fact that they weren't on the south shore might give them a false sense of security thinking the agents searching for them wouldn't search there. Just as Foster had thought. But Gilbert surely hadn't alerted just Foster to the situation. Or he would shortly inform whoever needed to be informed as soon as Foster told him what he had witnessed.

Anger suddenly filled Foster. These were his lands, too. He was a Northcott, even if he was the third-born son. It enraged him to think that someone thought so little of his family that they would put them at risk this way. And what of the smugglers' friends and family? If they were from these parts, and even if they weren't, they were in danger if the smugglers were caught and arrested, which they certainly would be if Foster had any say in the matter.

His blood ran cold, and all his muscles froze into stillness when he suddenly heard the snap of a twig behind him. He knew he hadn't sufficiently concealed himself, but he had thought the risk was minimal since he was surely invisible from below.

"Frost?"

It was little more than a rustle of wind on the air, but he knew instantly that it was Daisy. He had been just thinking about dodging her. Had he conjured her with his thoughts? Trying to make no noise or at least as little as possible, Foster wiggled out of the small space he had wedged himself into, righteous indignation warring with the feeling of being wrong-footed being caught in such a position by the beautiful young woman.

"What in the name of all that's holy are you doing here?" It took all his ability and self-control not to bellow the question at the foolish girl.

"I couldn't sleep and heard you leave, so I followed you."

"Are you daft?" He hadn't been able to keep as quiet with that demand. He quickly pulled her down into a crouch behind the boulder he had been trying to hide beside. He stared down into the cove anxiously, but it seemed the smugglers were still preoccupied with their own activities. Or perhaps the wind that was starting to grow wilder had carried his words away for him.

"What are you doing out here, Frost? Are you involved in the smuggling trade?" Daisy sounded incredulous but firmly disapproving.

Foster could only be relieved that she was keeping her voice low. He was surprised that she seemed to have perceived the full situation with just a glance. Or maybe she had been watching him for some time and he hadn't noticed. With a shake of his head, he dismissed that thought. He seemed to have a strange sixth sense where she was concerned. It was next to impossible that she could have been nearby and he hadn't noticed.

"No, I'm not involved in smuggling. How preposterous."

"More preposterous than finding you hanging over a cliff and smugglers below? Why else would you be here?"

"I'm not involved with them. I'm trying to figure out what to do about them."

She stared at him with wide eyes and a closed mouth, as though she were too stunned to have a comeback.

"Why?" she breathed the word, carefully keeping her sound to the barest minimum.

"Does it matter why? You need to leave, Miss Alcott. You are only endangering us both, in a very real way."

"They surely cannot see or hear us all the way up here like we are," she protested.

"Do you really care to take that chance? I saw very real guns on their person when they got out of their boats."

She started to rise to see for herself, and Foster quickly pulled her down to the ground next to him, evoking a small gasp from her.

"Stop manhandling me, Foster Northcott. Your father would have you by the ear for your treatment of a lady."

"I rather suspect he would have *you* by the ear for traipsing about the moors in the middle of the night. He would be more likely to flail you with his tongue for being so foolish as to court being compromised."

His words seemed to take her aback. "Compromised? How can I be compromised?"

"Are you really this foolish, Daisy? You were never wont to be."

He watched in fascination as what appeared to be very hot colour splashed up her cheeks, leading Foster to suppose she was either embarrassed or angry. Or maybe even both.

"Unless you're trying to entrap me into marriage," Foster then speculated in a cool tone.

She quickly stifled her gasp of outrage, but it was enough to have them both cowering by the boulder in the hopes that she hadn't drawn the attention of the criminals below. Her wildly widened eyes staring at him would have been amusing if they weren't dealing with a situation that carried real danger with it. He was relieved that she seemed to realize the situation they were in to at least a certain extent. Behind the fear in her gaze, he could also sense regret for engaging him in conversation when they were facing an actual threat.

Finally, after what seemed like an eternity but was probably only a minute or two, Foster lifted his head slightly to survey the smugglers in the cove. They appeared to be finished unloading their shipment and stowing it in a cave high enough on the beach that the tide wouldn't reach it. As he watched, they pushed their boat back into the river and started rowing vigorously, no longer as concerned about silence.

If he didn't have Daisy to contend with, he would make his way down to the beach and find out conclusively what they were trading in. But he did have Daisy to deal with. He couldn't prolong the nightly encounter.

"It doesn't appear that we are about to be killed for your foolishness."

"My foolishness," she hissed at him in outrage. "I wasn't the one who suggested I had any desire to be wed with you. That you would think I would want anyone to be trapped into marriage with me is beyond my ability to comprehend your stupidity."

"Now you're just being mean," Foster said with a laugh as he pulled her along toward the rough trail they had evidently both travelled to arrive at the cove.

"Why didn't you ride?" he asked. "Are you not going to be exhausted after this?"

He turned to watch her reaction when he asked the question. Her expressive face usually told him far more than she would ever openly admit. A myriad of conflicting emotions chased themselves over her features. Her mouth tightened as though she were biting back a retort, but her eyes couldn't quite meet his gaze.

"I couldn't ride, as a horse would make too much noise. Besides, I couldn't ride without a saddle in my skirts," she stated calmly. "I'm exhausted already. So yes, I'm sure to be intensely tired tomorrow. But I couldn't abide my curiosity. I had to know what you've been up to."

"What did you suspect me of? Why did you think my whereabouts were any of your concern?"

While he watched her, even though he couldn't see very clearly in the dim moonlight, it was evident that colour ebbed and flowed on her face. And suddenly, the fierce young woman he had known for years, who seemed much larger than she actually was, seemed to shrink before his watchful gaze as her shoulders slumped and her steps shortened.

"I don't know what I suspected you of specifically; I was just suspicious. You were acting strangely. You are quite correct; it was none of my concern. But I thought you might be about to bring scandal or shame upon Amelia, and I couldn't allow that to happen."

"Instead, *you* are going to bring it upon her; is that what you are after? Did you not think you ought to bring your concerns to the viscount or our father rather than to put yourself at risk this way?"

"I could never go to your father about anything!" Daisy's appalled expression at the very thought was almost enough to bring a niggle of amusement to the situation. Almost, but not quite. This was far too serious, and she had put their lives in jeopardy, besides their unmarried state.

Foster merely stared at her, enjoying the discomfort he could see she was in. She should have thought of that before she followed him on this fool's errand.

"Please elaborate on how you thought to confirm your suspicions without compromising either of us and still return to the house undetected. You have surely already been gone from the house for at least an hour. It will be another thirty or forty minutes before you could possibly be tucked back into your bed. It would be scandalous enough if you were found in the library searching for a book to pass a restless night. No one will think you are innocent if you are found to be wandering the heath in the middle of the night."

"I had meant to follow you in the morning. But I kept thinking I wouldn't possibly awake early enough, so I couldn't sleep. And then I saw you from my window, and I followed you."

Foster was appalled. He would never have thought anyone had observed him, let alone a gently bred young woman. It was a good thing he had no interest in a life as an agent for the Home Office. He was obviously no good at it. He offered her a stern glare for her troubles before turning on his heel and tramping back toward the house. He hadn't been exaggerating when he mentioned the distance and time. With her encumbered by skirts and them both already being tired by the late-night excursion, it was likely to be closer to an hour before they could regain their rooms.

And that was if they remained undetected. Foster was no longer familiar with the servants' schedules. There were sure to be footmen set for security as well as some servants beginning to stir for their duties. While he could swear them to secrecy, he didn't count on their loyalty to him, nor anyone's ability to keep such a juicy secret to themselves.

"Don't be a worried old nurserymaid, Frost. I have been gadding about undetected my whole life. No one will ever know I was out and about; I can assure you."

He remained unconvinced. But she didn't hold him back. Foster was nearing exhaustion due to several short nights in a row. But Daisy was able to keep pace with him, as though she weren't the least bit tired. A glance at her face told him that was untrue. The dim light of the moon showed him that she had what looked like light bruises under her eyes and her mouth that had once been so pinched with her outrage, now appeared slack from fatigue. He almost smiled at the gentle vision.

"Did you see anything noteworthy? Was it worth the risk you took?"

"What are you talking about?"

She actually sounded confused. Foster almost laughed. But then he sighed.

"You left the house in the middle of the night to follow me because you were feeling suspicious. Did you see what you wanted to see?"

Her chin lifted, and she no longer looked so tired.

"Now that you mention it, I have no idea what I was seeing. It looked like you were following suspicions of your own. There were men with guns and ugly looking knives. But it didn't appear as though you were a part of whatever they were up to. You were observing them. Are you a tax man, Foster?" Her eyes were wide, and she looked torn between awe and disgust. Foster bit back his amusement. Nobles had a complicated attitude toward smugglers. Which was why Gilbert had asked Foster to look into the matter rather than Lucian. Noblemen were so appreciative of their French brandy that they were willing to turn a blind eye to how it arrived on their shores.

"Did you think I was a part of the smuggling gang when you followed me?"

"That was not the first idea I had. I wouldn't have thought this would be the best location. If we were in Dorset or Sussex, I would have been far more suspicious of such activity."

"Which is probably why they chose Everleigh. Who would think to search for smugglers here?"

"What are you going to do about it? Is this why you've been leaving the house and acting so skittish?"

"I have not been acting skittish," Foster scoffed, offended at the thought.

Daisy laughed. "Perhaps skittish wasn't the right word. But you have been acting quite shady, you must admit."

"I admit no such thing, Miss Alcott."

His huffy tone brought another tinkle of laughter from the young woman at his side, and Foster found it impossible to hold onto his anger with her, even though she had been acting strangely herself.

"I still don't understand why you thought to take this upon yourself. Did you not realize you could be walking into a dangerous situation beyond your control? Do you make a habit of wandering the moors in the middle of the night and following strange men to possible assignations?"

Her face looked as though it were on fire, and Foster wouldn't have been the least bit surprised if she stamped her foot like a child.

"No, I do not make a habit of such behaviour," she insisted heatedly before her face suddenly transformed into a sheepish expression. "I know, it was exceedingly foolish of me. But you have always brought out the worst in me. I couldn't decide if I was merely being suspicious of you because it was you. So, I didn't want to involve anyone else in case it was something perfectly innocent."

"What sort of perfectly innocent activities can you think of that take place out of doors in the middle of the night?" Now Foster was curious about the workings of her mind.

Heat appeared to flood her face anew and she tried to stammer out a reply. "Well, perhaps innocent was the wrong word, but not nefarious. Perhaps perfectly normal would be a better way to phrase it."

"You are the strange one here, Miss Alcott. I don't think it's the least bit normal to be abroad at this hour. Any rational person would be abed at this time. Even by Town standards, I would expect."

"Surely not by Town standards," Daisy argued with a puff of laughter. "I don't think my brother ever goes to bed during the dark hours."

"Reed is an exception. And I wouldn't necessarily use 'rational' as a descriptor for him."

To his surprise, despite the insult he had just delivered to her brother, Daisy merely smiled and nodded. They walked along in almost companionable silence for a number of minutes before Daisy interrupted his thoughts.

"So, what do you plan to do about those men?" She began with that question, but her simple curiosity quickly turned to a frowning concern. "Why were you coming out here in search of them if you aren't a tax man? Did you not fear for your safety?"

"I've faced far more dangerous situations, Daisy," Foster countered in a dry tone, returning to his use of the familiar. "You do remember that I usually live in Upper Canada, don't you?"

His sarcasm brought a flush to her face, but her gaze didn't waver. Instead, she lifted a haughty eyebrow. If he weren't taller than her, she would certainly be staring down her elegant little nose at him.

"Are there many smugglers in the colonies, Frost?" she asked in an arctic tone.

"You cannot turn this upon me, Daisy. You were wrong to leave the comfort and safety of your bedchamber and follow me into the night. It doesn't matter why or what I was doing. It is none of your affair. Leave it be."

"Alcott isn't far from here," she persisted. "It is likely to be something Florent would be interested in. Or my father," she added as an afterthought.

"What makes you think they don't already know?"

Daisy blinked and stared. Foster was pleased to see a flicker of uncertainty dance across her features.

"Tell me what you have planned," she demanded even though there was less strength behind her bluster this time.

"Why should I? I don't want you anywhere near this situation, Daisy. Did you not see the weapons those men had? They do not appear to be the sort that would hesitate to use them."

Chapter Seven

Daisy was torn between fascination, terror, and exhaustion. Foster wasn't wrong. She was a dolt and had been courting disaster when she followed him. Even doing so in the early morning would have been questionable enough. Doing so in the wee hours like this was beyond the pale. It was the most thoughtless thing she had done in her life. She was fortunate he hadn't pushed her over the cliff. She had actually thought he might when he first spied her approaching from behind him.

She should have realized it might be something actually dangerous. But reason was never one of the strongest factors in her interactions with Foster Northcott. Not since they'd met when she was barely more than a toddler, but especially not since the lake incident. When she was a child, she had hero worshipped Frost but since the incident, Daisy had hated him with a determined effort. So, the thought of him being up to something questionable had made her gleeful.

Instead, he was trying to protect his family's reputation. Or something. He wouldn't actually tell her. But whatever it was, it wasn't something she ought to have put her nose into. But now that she had, she couldn't very well unsee what she had seen.

"Are you investigating them, Frost? Are you going to see what it is they hid in the cave? Do you know who they are? Are you going to tell Adelaide or Everleigh?"

"You have way more questions than I have answers. And I'm far too tired to deal with your curiosity tonight. You have to stay out of it."

"I can't."

Foster's face might have been carved from granite as he stared at her without expression for the length of several heart beats.

"What do you mean you can't?"

Daisy shrugged. "You might be right that I shouldn't have involved myself, but I did. I know there's something going on, and I cannot allow you to come to harm."

"Yes, you can," he insisted before allowing a soft bark of laughter to sound from his throat, but it didn't really sound like amusement. "And I shan't come to harm without your involvement, I can assure you. I'm much more likely to do so if you don't leave it alone. Not the least of my danger would be from the hands of your brothers if I were to allow you to get mixed up in this."

"I would like to know how you think you could stop me," she said softly as though she were actually curious about the matter.

Another short bark of laughter from her companion put her teeth on edge, but he quickly sobered.

"Daisy Alcott, swear to me that you won't go there on your own," Foster demanded abruptly, as though he just realized that it was a very real possibility.

"I don't need to promise you anything," Daisy countered.

"I'll get your brothers involved if you don't start showing some reasonableness."

"Foster Northcott, I never knew you to be a tattle tale."

Foster shrugged. "I've never had to be. But you are acting daft and cannot be left to run about the countryside chasing after smugglers."

Daisy tried to appear unconcerned over his words. "Go ahead. My brothers shan't care overmuch. They know better than to stick their noses into my activities."

"Daisy," Foster began in a warning tone. "I am no longer jesting with you. This is a serious and dangerous matter. It is not a matter to be involving a gently bred female."

"Since we're neighbours, I would think you could see that it is just as much my business as it is yours."

Suddenly, before she could even blink or draw a deep breath, Foster had her clasped tightly by the arms and he was giving her a slight shake.

"Don't be more daft than usual, Daisy." His low voice was probably meant to sound menacing but to the contrary, Daisy felt the heat of attraction curl low in her belly. It was not unpleasant. She had to bite her lip not to smile at his attempt to intimidate her into doing his bidding. A part of her wanted to melt into his embrace. But he wasn't trying to embrace her, and the realization of her reactions caused her to stiffen in his grasp.

"Unhand me, Mr. Northcott," she demanded in as cool a tone as she could muster under the circumstances. "And might I add, I've never been daft, and well you know it."

"You are being quite daft right now," he insisted but there was less heat in his voice, and he suddenly let her go as though he had just realized that he had grabbed her in the first place. "And you're making me daft with you," he finished, a note of disgust sounding in his tone. "We really must hurry. I shan't marry you for your troubles if that was what you were hoping with this mad escapade of yours."

Daisy gasped in outrage. "I would never try to entrap any man into marriage, least of all you," she declared hotly.

"Prove it by getting yourself to your room without ruining yourself in the process," he insisted, his voice as cold as his hard gaze she noticed when she glanced at him from beneath her eyelashes.

She couldn't have even begun to fathom why he would be so distant and angry with her. There was every possibility she could have helped him if something had gone wrong when he was watching the smugglers. What if he had been shot or accosted in some way? Surely, he shouldn't have been out there alone anyway. He ought to be thanking her for her interference.

Daisy nearly snorted. Even she wasn't so simple minded as to believe that particular tale. She lengthened her stride. There was no way for her to know just how much time had passed since she had left her room. She hadn't lied when she said she had no interest in entrapping a man into being her husband, especially not Foster Northcott. Frost was right. She needed to be well ensconced in her room long before anyone else in the house stirred. With a house this full of servants and guests it would be a feat if she managed it.

It was one more reason to feel that life was unfair. Why was it perfectly acceptable for Foster to be wandering about at any hour, but she could be ruined if anyone were to hear of her absence? It wouldn't do any good to lament the state of affairs. But she was nearly running back to the house as though her thoughts were chasing her. It was only Foster's chuckle as though he knew he had gotten under her skin that kept her from picking up her skirts and actually making a run for it.

Daisy removed her shoes as soon as they got inside the kitchen door and crept after his large silent shape.

A part of her wanted to insist she could make it on her own, but she wouldn't allow herself to be that foolish. It would be the least risky to allow Foster to help her make it as quickly as possible. He surely would also know how to melt into the shadows if they were to encounter a footman on patrol.

A sigh of relief was the only sound she made as she shut the door on blessedly silent hinges, turning the key in the lock for good measure. Her maid wouldn't bother her until a fair bit later. Daisy was certain of it as she had assured the girl that she intended to sleep in due to the expectation of a later night the next day.

She made quick work of undressing herself and slipping into the nightgown she had thrown onto the bed. Daisy almost climbed up onto the bed before she realized it would be odd for her to leave her gown out like that. It would give her away for sure. There were always details that needed to be attended to. She nearly grumbled at the thought, but fatigue was pulling her under. She hurried to right her room, ensuring she had left no evidence to point at her midnight expedition. It took the very last of her energy to snuggle under the covers and close her eyes.

In what felt like mere minutes but must have been hours by the slant of the light when she finally opened her eyes to the bright new day, it was time to arise. The scratching at the door that must have been what woke her up sounded again, and Daisy remembered that she had locked the door. She swallowed down all her reactions – the fear at the possibility of being caught as well as the laughter that welled within her at her own audacity.

She slipped from the bed and hurried to the door.

"Oh, Miss, why was your door locked? I didn't think I'd be waking you this late."

"I'm sorry, Frannie. I had a strange feeling last night for some reason and felt the need to lock it. But it's good that you woke me. I don't usually sleep this late."

Daisy couldn't meet her maid's watchful gaze, so she turned back toward the bed but didn't climb the stairs back into it. It was merely to give herself something else to focus on.

"Should I fetch you a tray? It's late enough that there isn't likely to be anyone left in the breakfast room."

"Oh dear, am I really that late?" Now Daisy was feeling even more ashamed of her nighttime expedition.

"Most of the other ladies have ordered trays. You aren't the only one stalling this morning."

Daisy wanted to sputter that she wasn't dawdling, but that would raise far too many questions, so she managed to stem her response, merely sending the maid down to the kitchens for the promised tray. While she waited, she wandered around the lovely room she had been allotted at Everleigh House and pondered the experience of the house party thus far.

This was her third day in residence but most everyone else had just arrived. It had been wise of Amelia to invite her and her mother early like that so they could acclimatize to the setting before there were even more guests in residence. It made Daisy feel particularly cared for by her friends.

So then why was she running about the countryside in the middle of the night chasing a man she disliked so intensely and getting herself caught up in a smuggling operation? She supposed she must be just as daft as Frost said she was. She would never admit that to him, of course, but he was likely right.

Sitting down with a bit of a plop at the mirrored table in her room, Daisy studied her reflection, hoping to find the source of her disquiet reflected there for all to see. She didn't look any different than usual aside from obviously not quite enough sleep. She hoped her maid brought coffee on the tray; she couldn't very well claim to need a nap after having awoken at such a late hour. That would lead to all sorts of questions she had no desire to answer.

A deeper survey showed Daisy the excitement shining in her eyes. Apparently, she thrived on danger and intrigue. What was Foster up to? She tried to shake her head at herself but then rolled her eyes. Her reflection wasn't going to listen to her. Daisy only hoped she had enough forethought to be able to avoid a scandal. She started to fidget as she waited and so strode toward the wardrobe to decide on her day's attire. She didn't usually care what she wore and left that decision to Frannie. But boredom and the need to set herself on the right path were combining to push her in the direction of taking a hand in her own toilette.

She was just starting to really rifle through her gowns when Frannie arrived back in her room.

"Oh, Miss, you aren't rumpling anything are you?" The maid called out to her anxiously before clamping her mouth shut in consternation. "I apologize, Miss Daisy. You can do whatever you'd like." She bobbed a curtsey and Daisy laughed.

"I was bored, Frannie, I'm sorry to say. But I don't think I mussed anything up. I was trying to decide what I ought to wear. But you make it look so easy, and I haven't a clue where to start."

Frannie laughed even as she guided her mistress toward the small seating area where she had placed the tray.

"You eat and I'll sort it out. Do you know which activities you are likely to be involved in today?"

"This afternoon we're to play shuttlecock and things like that out of doors if the weather holds fair.

Tomorrow we're to go driving and riding in the surrounding countryside, but Amelia thought people would wish for a day without travel."

Frannie made a hum of acknowledgment even as she was carefully sorting through her mistress' garments and accessories.

Before long, Daisy was fed, coifed, dressed, and on her way. There was already a rising murmur of voices coming from one of the receiving rooms she had explored the morning before while they waited for the others to arrive.

"Miss Alcott, you look fresh and lovely this morning," Lord Merton greeted her as soon as she stepped into the room, making her question his eyesight. But her amusement allowed her to pleasantly accept his words as the compliment he intended. One could argue that he was merely being polite by not mentioning how tired she looked. Or even that he was wise. Just her looking so tired could call her reputation into question, she supposed with a quiet sigh.

Forbidding her gaze from searching out Foster, Daisy made her way through the room, greeting and speaking with all her fellow guests without looking around the room to see who else was there. She supposed it was far more polite that way anyway. Finally, she reached her mother who stared at her with a frown. Daisy could see that Mama thought to question her fatigue. Before she could, though, Daisy gave her a wide, bright smile.

"Good morning, my lady. You look fresh and sparkling this morning. How do you do?"

It was as though Lady Alcott wasn't certain how to answer her daughter, so she only lifted an eyebrow at her youngest child, filled with suspicion over her actions and attitude but clearly not prepared to question her about it.

"I am well, thank you, my dear," she finally answered before patting the seat next to her. "Do sit down and tell me how you found your breakfast this morning. My maid informed me you had a tray brought to your room much like most of the women, but I thought it was a trifle out of character."

Daisy made the effort to appear as unconcerned as possible, grinning at her mother and leaning in closer as though to share a secret. "I figured I might as well take advantage of the opportunity for decadence."

This brought a light flow of laughter from those who overheard which tinged Daisy's cheeks with heat, but she thought it was the best tack to take on the matter. She knew her mother wouldn't necessarily be fooled by her glib answer, but she also wouldn't question her publicly.

Lord Simmons approached and sat on her other side. "Miss Alcott, are you an experienced player at the games her ladyship has planned for the day?"

Daisy turned to him with a smile trying not to think about Foster's assessment of this gentleman being the perfect match for her.

"I am," Daisy answered with a smile before widening it and elaborating. "Or rather we could say that I used to be. I cannot say that I've played any of the ones I think she's planning in quite some time. As the youngest of my siblings, there was no one to play with after a while."

"Are your brothers no longer in residence? I thought they all still called Alcott home."

Daisy kept her smile in place when she really wanted to frown over his questioning. "My oldest brother is kept quite busy assisting our father with the running and expanding of the estate. My middle brother has a home of his own, and my youngest brother has been continuing his studies. So, none of them are prepared to entertain me overmuch. Besides, the lot of us are far too competitive to remain in good humour with one another if we were to make an attempt at our childhood games."

"So, are we in for a rousing fight this afternoon, then?" he asked with amusement that Daisy couldn't quite identify. Was he making a jest of her? Or was he genuinely amused by her and her siblings' rivalry?

Daisy lifted a shoulder and shook her head hoping it appeared as though she too were amused at the thought. "I have grown up quite a bit since last I played shuttlecock. I am unlikely to hit anyone with my racquet. At least not intentionally." She added this last bit in an effort to cause further amusement for the others. She still hadn't heard if her brother would be joining the house party. If he did, it was entirely possible that the household would be treated to a fierce competition after all. Daisy suspected that might not display her in the most advantageous way. But still Lord Simmons appeared content to sit at her side and wasn't trying to hurry away.

"What about you, my lord? Are you an experienced player?"

"Not terribly," he admitted. "I only played at school. And I was far from the best player. Gilbert Northcott was the best and didn't mind rubbing it in all the other boys' faces."

"Never say so," Daisy countered with a laugh. "I wouldn't have thought that fine gentleman would be so mean."

"Boys can be quite monstrous," the viscount replied from her side.

"It would seem so. Of course, I do know that from my brothers, but I thought they might be unique. Especially my brother, Reed."

"Not in the least," Lord Simmons answered immediately. "I don't know Reed well, but your brothers Florent and Laurence were at school at the same time as I was, and I can assure you, they were only nearly as competitive as the Northcott brothers."

"And yet you all seem to remain friends," Daisy marvelled.

Lord Simmons nodded, smiled, and lifted one shoulder elegantly all at once in a remarkable display of nonchalance. "One must tolerate the vagaries of one's fellow man."

This drew laughter from everyone within earshot. It also gave Daisy the excuse she was looking for to allow her eyes to stray. She knew she was searching for Foster and hated the weakness, trying to excuse that she was in need of an explanation for the night before. Was he involved? Who should they tell? The earl? A magistrate? The local squire? Daisy thought to send a message to her father, but how could she explain how she had come by the knowledge? And really, what knowledge did she even have? Very little when one thought on the matter.

Frustration welled within her. Throughout the morning, Lords Merton and Simmons vied for her attention, and she could not enjoy the experience. She tried to get to know Lady Isabelle, but that young woman was quieter than Daisy had expected and didn't make it easy in Daisy's distracted state. Everyone, including her two best friends, did their best to keep each other entertained. Her fellow guests were more than convivial yet Daisy could not get into the spirit of the jests and games. It was most disheartening, and she knew herself for a fool. She hoped the promised arrival of the slightly scandalous Lady Constance might bring the needed distraction she was seeking. From what she had heard about the woman, Daisy was looking forward to getting to know her better. While Daisy considered herself to be conventional, she was deeply curious about the woman who had chosen to flout convention altogether.

Chapter Eight

Foster was growing frustrated with the hordes of people his sisters-in-law had packed into his childhood home. He understood it wasn't his, that he didn't have a home of his own yet, but still he felt proprietorial. While he had the financial ability to buy a property, he didn't want to yet. It had never bothered him before but suddenly, being in his old home and not feeling "at home" made him feel rootless and unsettled. And he wished they would all leave. Or he wished he had never come back. He ought to be negotiating with natives and trading pelts or digging for minerals or panning for gold or building fences somewhere, anywhere, doing anything but sitting in a fussily decorated parlor with a too tight cravat listening to fashionable people who knew nearly nothing talk about subjects that mattered so little to him.

If his brother hadn't asked him to be there, he certainly would have been elsewhere. But there were smugglers on Everleigh lands. And even if he would never inherit and therefore it wasn't really his, Everleigh was Northcott land. He was a Northcott. It was very, very personal.

His gaze scanned the room. No one there was of any interest to him. Even his new sisters were failing to keep his attention. His gaze was ensnared by Daisy Alcott and his breath stuttered in his chest. Perhaps there were some things of interest in the room. With a blink, Daisy tore her gaze away, and Frost felt it like a punch to his midsection before he shook his head to rid himself of the foolish thoughts.

He could not allow the chit to involve herself in something so dangerous. But he knew it would be nearly impossible to stop her. She had been inquisitive as a child and a pest as a girl. Now, as a grown woman, he was afraid she might be conniving on top of her intelligence; what a dreadful combination for a man's peace of mind.

Perhaps he ought to tell his brother, Lucian, or one of Daisy's brothers. Reed came to mind. The lazy lout should have come to the house party and then he could have seen to his sister. But Reed was off hunting with his friends and Frost couldn't see himself confiding in Daisy's oldest brother. That man was so serious and proper, Foster couldn't imagine what he would do to his sister if he were to find out she was courting scandal.

Or perhaps he ought to solve the dilemma of the smugglers while she was busy making cow's eyes at Lord Merton and Lord Simmons.

Foster knew he was being unfair. He had even suggested to Daisy that Simmons would be a good match for her. He shouldn't fault her for following through on his suggestion. He was well aware that she wasn't even flirting, not like many London ladies often did. She was just being herself. Her usual intelligent, friendly self. The self he had always wished to keep for himself. Until he had broken their friendship and made her hate him with a fierceness that was her way of doing everything.

How was he going to keep her out of the caves?

Foster got to his feet, pacing to the tall windows that opened onto the terrace overlooking the back gardens. It was such a beautiful estate. This was why he had returned when asked, even though he had any number of other places to be. Nothing was ever as beautiful to him as Everleigh.

The murmur of conversation ebbed and flowed behind him, but it was as though it had disappeared as Foster looked out over his ancestral home. His forebears had certainly had grandiose ambitions he thought with a grin as his peripheral vision took in the wide sprawl of the two wings of the house. No wonder the servants at Everleigh always had to be young, just getting around the house would take much of their energy, let alone being able to take care of whatever tasks were included in their jobs.

"Are you going to go see what they brought?"

The whispered words came from behind almost making him start in surprise.

"Miss Alcott, you shouldn't be telling secrets with me when you have beaux to entertain."

She shrugged, not taking her eyes from where his gaze had been fixed – out to the moors where the cliffs hid the caves where they knew the smugglers had stashed whatever they had to hide.

"It isn't any of our affair, Miss Alcott," Foster insisted, ignoring the frown that darkened her brow. He could see she wished to argue with him, but she swallowed her response. That impressed him. The girl had indeed grown up. She never would have been able to swallow her anger like that as a girl.

"I understand, Mr. Northcott. Thank you for reminding me."

Foster's jaw almost dropped open. Daisy Alcott was lying to him. He never would have thought she had it in her. But he couldn't very well accuse her of such in front of the gathered guests. And she was saying the right words. He ought to be pleased. But he wasn't. A giant morass of problems yawned at his feet, and he didn't see his way around it.

To his surprise, she returned to the conversation that was swirling around the room as though she hadn't even stepped out of it. That took remarkable skill and attention. Even he wouldn't have been able to do so, and he was one who prided himself on never losing the thread of a conversation.

The party broke up a little as Amelia directed her guests into various pursuits. It would be the perfect time for him to escape to the bluffs. No one would know for certain where anyone else might be. So, no one's absence would be noted. Or so he hoped. He went to the stables to have a horse saddled.

It was a glorious late autumn day, and he was looking forward to the ride. The horse that was led to him appeared just as anxious to go as he was. It would be perfect. He allowed the horse to show his paces and they quickly ate up the ground, but Foster had to rein him in when they got closer to the cliffs. The terrain of the moors could become quite unpredictable.

When he got near to the cove in which he had seen the smugglers the night before, Foster was surprised to see two other horses tethered to a small shrub. Further examination brought colourful curses to his mind. Daisy was making her way down the edge of the cliff with what appeared to be an Everleigh groom in tow.

"That woman is going to be the death of me." He set off in intentional pursuit of the pair.

A few minutes later he was surprised at how quick and sure-footed Daisy evidently was. But she also seemed to be oblivious to his approach until he got close enough to call out to her. It was obvious she hadn't just been ignoring him when she uttered a small shriek and nearly lost her footing. The quick-acting groom reached out to steady her.

"Foster Northcott, you nearly gave me apoplexy. What are you doing here?"

"I could very well demand of you the same thing. Shouldn't you be back at the house enjoying my sister's hospitality?"

Daisy flushed to her roots and appeared suddenly bashful despite her continued descent to the shore below. Even though she had brought a groom with her, she obviously wanted to keep him in the dark about why she was there as she kept her voice just loud enough for Foster to hear. "I just couldn't stay away, Frost, surely you understand since you are here, too. You know you want to know what's inside. I just couldn't stand not knowing. And I didn't trust that you'd tell me if you came without me."

"So, you decided to come by yourself?" He was incredulous. "Would you have told me if I didn't catch you out for myself?"

Again, she flushed, and he would have found it charming if he didn't also wish to throttle her. "Are you so eager to court scandal, Daisy?"

"Not in the least," she countered hotly. "I have a groom with me, as would be expected. How was I to know you'd be here, too?"

"There could be far worse awaiting you here than me, you silly female."

"I'm not being silly, Mr. Northcott," she returned with ice in her tone. "I have just as much right to be here as you do."

"These are not your family's lands, Miss Alcott," he argued.

"Perhaps not, but ours aren't far off, and what goes on here will affect my people as much as yours."

"Why didn't you just tell your brothers?"

Daisy appeared as though she were going to ignore his question as she completed the final descent to the beach but as soon as she hopped the last short distance, she turned and watched him make his way quickly down. She planted her hands on her hips and appeared as though she were going to give him a dressing down but then she grinned.

"Can you believe I wanted to keep them safe? I didn't want them to worry. At least not Florent. My other brothers might think it a lark, but neither of them are here. Laurence has his own property to concern himself with and Reed is too busy trying to prove he isn't jealous of his brothers. But Florent is far too preoccupied with Alcott as it is. I think he's already burning up with concerns he doesn't have any desire to share with his baby sister. And then I also know he wouldn't share any of the adventure with me."

She looked so adorably sheepish over that last statement that he had to laugh even though he shouldn't want to share it with her either.

"And so, you decided to keep it all for yourself?"

She shrugged. "I would have told someone, probably Adelaide, if I were to find anything of importance. I have no way of knowing what exactly I saw last night, and there is no easy way to tell anyone what I saw, either. I sort of figured that you would tell anyone who needed telling. So, this was my only chance to see for myself." She paused as though things were suddenly dawning on her and her hands, which she had slowly relaxed, were suddenly perched fiercely upon her slim hips once more. "Why are you here, Foster? Why are you here alone, to be exact? Why didn't *you* tell Adelaide and leave it for him to tell whoever needs telling? Or are you involved in this, as I suspected last night?"

Foster threw his head back and laughed.

"You still hate me, don't you? Do you actually think I've turned into a pirate since I left home? That I'm in league with smugglers and am using my father's lands for my crimes?"

His laughter had embarrassed her, but she just shrugged and continued to stare at him in defiance, as though daring him to say something more. Suddenly her eyes widened, and she clamped a hand over her mouth to hide its dropping open.

"You don't suspect that Adelaide or Everleigh are involved, do you? Is that why you haven't told? You want to know what's being smuggled just as much as I do, don't you?"

The chit was too smart by half. And he would rather rip out his own tongue than tell her such.

"Why would you suspect my father or brother of being in league with criminals?" he demanded, making her bristle.

"In league is quite a strong statement, Mr. Northcott. I thought it possible they might be turning a blind eye in exchange for a couple bottles, if it's that sort of product being moved through these parts."

"Is that why you didn't say anything?"

"You are being more ridiculous than necessary, Foster, and well you know it. How could I have possibly said anything? I can just envision that conversation. Would you have me tell your father, 'pardon me, my lord, the earl, I just so happened to be walking on the bluffs in the middle of the night and stumbled upon a gang up to no good.' What do you think he would have to say then?"

"You needn't get so high and mighty sounding, Daisy. I told you that you shouldn't have followed me."

"That is all well and good to remind me of now, well after the fact. But it doesn't change that it's already done. And now you are the one who has followed me, so you're just as bad or worse than I am."

"I didn't follow you, you ridiculous gudgeon. I just so happened to want to see for myself as well."

Daisy stared at him as though she didn't quite believe him, but then she burst into laughter that she attempted not to allow to get out of hand. Sound could ricochet off the bluffs and carry quite far over the water. Given the very real possibility of violent criminals being about, Foster was pleased to see she had gained her senses and was trying not to make too much noise.

"We are quite the pair, aren't we, Frost? I'm not sure what is to become of us at this rate, so we'd best be quick about it. We've already wasted far too much time with our arguments. Why don't we just get on with it? We both want to know what's in there. Let's gird our loins and go see."

Foster couldn't help grinning over her wording. She had always been a complete hand. And she was right. They had come this far and needed to get on with it. If they were going to try to spare themselves from scandal, they needed to be back to the house as quickly as possible. And the fact that she had a groom in tow just might protect her. Not if they were found together, but she was unlikely to court disaster if they returned to the house separately. Somehow, she had managed to involve the least curious servant in the household. The groom didn't appear in the least interested in their conversation nor in their exploration. As soon as Foster had shown up, the groom had found a fallen log to sit upon and appeared to be nearly falling asleep. He wasn't the best one to be watching out for a young woman, but at least he wouldn't be carrying tales back to Everleigh. Or so he hoped.

He offered her his hand to help her over the rough ground ahead. She stared at it suspiciously for a moment but then grasped it tightly with a small smile. Foster's heart fluttered in his chest, and he wondered for a moment if he were becoming ill. Or perhaps he was losing his mind. Daisy Alcott could do that to a man, it would seem.

She wouldn't allow him to stand about wool gathering, though, as she stepped briskly toward the cave despite the unstable ground beneath their feet. The smugglers had certainly chosen a place hard to reach. They weren't the stupidest criminals he'd ever heard of, that was for certain. And that thought made him hesitate at the mouth of the cave, a fact for which Daisy took advantage, stepping inside before him. He shouldn't have allowed that. What if there had been someone left behind to guard the loot? He pulled her back against his chest, making her squeak quietly.

"What are you doing, Frost?" she whispered the question fiercely, bringing a smile to his face. She sounded like a furious mouse.

"I shouldn't have allowed you to go first."

"Why not? You always want that honor for yourself?"

"No, you rabbit, I didn't want you stepping into danger unknowingly," he whispered into her ear, holding her close even as he wanted to shove her behind him, out of the possibility of harm's way.

She was so close that he could feel the shiver that went through her. It wasn't cold enough to be a chill, he realized when he glanced down at her in question. She was staring at him with her eyes flared and her lips parted. Almost as though she were awaiting his kiss. Heat flooded him. All he could think about were her lips and how soft they looked as she stared at him with her chin slightly loosened and her eyelashes batting gently.

Without further thought, his head was lowering toward hers and their breath intermingled. His ears began to buzz, and a delicious tremble was felt low in his belly.

Just before their lips touched, she reached her palms onto his chest. It felt delicious. He took a deep breath, about to seal their lips together when she nearly knocked the breath right out of him with a mighty shove.

Chapter Nine

"**W**hat do you think you're doing, Foster Northcott?" she demanded in a louder than necessary voice filled with outrage.

"Be quiet," he hissed at her.

Daisy rolled her eyes. "I've already seen that the cave is empty aside from whatever is covered back in that corner. But there are no people here. And there was nowhere outside in which to hide. So, I could yell and scream at you and only we would have an earache from it. And I have half a mind to do so except that here in this cave it wouldn't be just you who suffered. What on God's green earth were you thinking?"

Pink highlighted his cheekbones as he bashfully kicked at the ground for the briefest moment before he wiped his face of all expression and stared at her as though he hadn't a clue what she was on about.

"I wasn't doing anything, Miss Alcott. I needed to be certain you weren't going to make noise in case there was someone in here."

A wave of indecision swept through Daisy before she bolstered her confidence.

"You are a liar, Foster Northcott, just as you've always been. You were going to kiss me. We both know it."

"How would you know such a thing?" Foster demanded. "Aren't you supposed to be the innocent one here?"

The heat that had been generated within her when Foster's lips had almost brushed against hers was quickly dissipating. It had been the most delicious but confusing sensation which had made her react almost violently. Overreact was a better word for it. She probably should have allowed it to play out, for now she would never know how it might have been.

For all his irritating ways, Daisy did trust Foster for the most part. She still hadn't forgiven him for leaving her to drown when she was a girl, but she knew he was a gentleman, deep down. So, she should have let him kiss her.

He was unfortunately accurate when he said she was the innocent party. She had still not yet received a kiss anywhere other than her wrist from any man. It was disheartening that she had overreacted quite so badly at the first opportunity. If only she could take back the last minute. Disappointment welled in the pit of her stomach. But, of course, she couldn't let Foster know that. With a sigh that she hoped remained mostly silent, she gave him another little push so he would let her through into the surprisingly large cave. She could stand comfortably while Foster only had to stoop slightly.

Curiosity filled her, and she wished she could explore every nook and cranny of the space, but time was quickly passing, and Daisy knew she would be missed if she didn't return to the house soon. Besides, the groom, no matter how inattentive he might wish to be, would surely bestir himself if she didn't return outside before long. She walked briskly toward the covered pile in the corner. She could barely make it out in the murky light cast by the angle of the sunlight streaming through the cave opening.

"Don't stand in the light, Frost, I can barely see a thing," she called out in complaint, prompting a snort from behind her that made her smile.

"You haven't learned a single thing during your years in Society, have you, my girl?"

"What sort of things?" she demanded even as she reached to pull back the covering. Foster reached around her to grab the other end.

"Like how to not be such a managing baggage," he replied with laughter sounding in his voice while they pulled back the heavy canvas.

"Is this a sail?" Daisy asked, curious about everything they were encountering.

"It would seem so," Foster agreed, still laughing. "Why are you dallying?" He asked when she was hesitating over pulling the cloth firmly from the pile.

"I'm nervous."

"Of what? You don't know how to be nervous," he added, making her smile and shake her head.

"There are various ramifications depending on what this is. And maybe we completely misconstrued what we saw last night and there's nothing nefarious here at all and we're about to violate someone's privacy."

"For one thing, Daisy, this is Everleigh land, so no one should be putting their private things here if they don't belong to Everleigh. That needn't even cross into your head. As to the first, I understand what you're saying but your curiosity got you this far, don't let it fail you now."

Daisy finally allowed all the pent-up feelings that had been accumulating to bubble over into hearty laughter even as she yanked the cloth firmly off the mound that was in front of them.

Cotton. Just as she had feared. Whiskey or brandy she could maybe dismiss. But someone was smuggling cotton through these parts. That would harm so many around, especially the poor tenants, she thought with a sigh. And Amelia's brother-in-law, too, she remembered. Never mind the gangs who wouldn't be far behind. Or were likely behind the entire escapade. They weren't likely to be able to get any magistrates to take on the case either.

"Who are the magistrates in these parts?" she asked, surprised to see a smile of approval upon Foster's face.

"You aren't a simpleton, that I'll grant you."

Daisy laughed. "That doesn't answer my question."

"I know as little as you evidently do," Foster answered, "even though we both grew up here," he added. "My father and brother most likely have some authority, but I don't think they're magistrates. What about your father?"

Daisy shook her head but shrugged feebly. "I would probably know if he was," she said with a laugh. "He takes his seat in the House, so I don't think he would have the availability to take matters of law into his hands around here." She sighed, not bothering to keep it silent. "Do you know who we ought to ask? Are you going to speak to Adelaide now? While I was inclined to think he might know about the liquid sort of smuggling, I truly don't believe any of our family members would be involved in this."

Foster dismissed Daisy's concerns, assuring her that she could safely leave the matters in his hands. He would look after it. Now that they knew it was cotton, the situation was even more dangerous than they had previously suspected.

She resisted his efforts to be rid of her at first but finally, with a sniff and a stomp, she turned on her heel, collected the footman who had clearly taken the time to nap, and climbed back up to where their horses were tethered.

Daisy couldn't really argue with Foster no matter how much she wished to. She should never have involved herself in the first place. She had been a simpleton to do so. And now she had to leave the matter with Foster or risk more than just scandal. As she rode away from the cliff with her inattentive groom in tow Daisy chewed on her lip and glanced back, wishing for one last glance of Foster. If he didn't leave the matter be, he faced danger for certain. She had to trust that he would make sure he had help the next time he returned to the cove.

Chapter Ten

Foster returned to the house in a much less hurried state than when he left. He was reluctant to rejoin the other guests as he really hated feeling like a guest in his childhood home. Everleigh ought to always be his home but that wasn't to be. He was well aware that he was always to visit. But that was what it would be – a visit – meaning a temporary stay, not somewhere he would live out the rest of his life.

Suddenly he wanted somewhere that represented roots and longevity. It was an uncomfortable realization to reach. He had been quite content to be a wanderer these last several years, striving to amass the fortune that would rival his younger brother's. Now he was starting to think that ambition was rather foolish. Surely, he had already collected enough to live comfortably. What was wrong with his inner workings that he had this overriding urge to have more than enough, to have a spectacular fortune, far more than Ashford? He loved his brother. Why did he feel the need to be better than him? And why was he suddenly questioning that need?

Daisy Alcott. A few days spent in the chit's company, and he was starting to have feelings and doubts and all manner of odd and unwelcome sensations.

The almost kiss wasn't necessarily an unwelcome sensation. Well, the sensations weren't unwelcome. The object of them was. Daisy? The most irritating female of his acquaintance? Why would she have to be the one he felt inclined to grow roots with?

It was merely being in this house, he assured himself. It was unsettling him. Reminding him of childhood experiences, most of which involved Daisy or members of her family. It wasn't her specifically. He was just feeling nostalgic. Once he got this matter of smugglers taken care of, he could get back on a ship and in six short weeks he would be back on more certain ground, pursuing his wealth, exactly the sort of situation he could fully comprehend, no complexities such as feelings need accompany him on the ship.

And how long could it possibly take to resolve this little matter? He didn't even need to resolve it, really. All he had to do was make sure it didn't get out of hand before Gilbert could return and take over. That was all. Days only. A week, at the most. Certainly, no more than a fortnight and he'd be well on his way.

With that reassuring thought revolving in his mind, Foster was able to insert himself neatly back into the fabric of his new sisters' party. No one observing him would know that he found everyone present insipid, and his thoughts were far removed from the odd little activities Amelia had decreed were absolutely necessary for the occasion.

When Daisy swept into the room he was in nearly an hour later, Foster tried to ignore the sense of relief that flooded him. He had started to worry about the girl. They had agreed that he would take a far more circuitous route to the house in order to ensure no one could surmise they had been absent together. Foster had begun to think that something had happened to delay her. Daisy ought to have been back before he was, since she had chosen the more direct route to the house, as she was the one at greater risk of censure for missing any of the party.

But when Foster didn't see her, he had thought she was somewhere else in the house. He hadn't realized just how concerned he was until she walked into the room.

She didn't actually just walk into the room. It was as though she burst into it with all her exuberance and energy vibrating around her. How was the chit to manage Society? No wonder she hadn't yet wed. It would take a special man to be able to appreciate and work with such a force as Daisy Alcott.

He could only hope her family was making an effort to ensure she was appropriately matched. But Foster was afraid that as the youngest of three girls, the family didn't see the urgency in the matter. They had already successfully married off two daughters, it didn't appear as though they were in any hurry to make arrangements for the third. Daisy Alcott should not be sitting on the sidelines of life.

And Foster Northcott was being a dolt.

He nearly laughed at the turn of his own thoughts. All these conflicting images were vying for his attention as she circulated through the room.

"Where have you been?" he hissed at her fiercely as she stopped near him, seemingly to watch the game play for a moment.

"Avoiding you," she returned with a lift of her pert little nose.

"Did anyone question your absence?"

"What absence, Mr. Northcott? I've been having a lovely morning visiting with friends and becoming better acquainted with those I have not previously known as well. Lady Constance and Miss Smith finally arrived and have fascinating tales to share," she added before slyly asking, "Did you miss me?"

She said it so sweetly and with such a direct expression that Foster actually, for the briefest moment, wondered if he had perhaps imagined the entire morning's excursion. But then she allowed one eyelid to droop over her eye in a quick, secret wink and his heart squeezed in his chest.

He didn't want to like her. He certainly didn't want to feel anything warmer than that. But he couldn't help admiring her spunk. She hadn't been able to resist involving herself in what she thought might be nefarious conduct on his part. It was laughable that she had suspected him. And beyond foolish that she involved herself in what could have been a dangerous expedition. But he couldn't really blame her. This was her home county. She rightly had a similarly possessive feeling toward it as he did. Even though, for both of them, the homes they grew up in weren't truly their homes. It was understandable that they both felt a strong urge to protect the people there from exploitation.

Because they *were* being exploited. Foster was confident neither his brother nor his father could possibly have any involvement in the illegal cotton trade. Foster was left to wonder what Gilbert's involvement was. It still shocked him that Gilbert was involved with the Home Office. But how did he know about the possibility of smuggling and yet hadn't been available to confirm it for himself? He supposed Gil must have heard something in some related investigation or other. Foster could only hope his brother would turn up soon so he could pass the responsibility on to someone else. All Foster wanted at this point was to get back on a swift westbound ship. At this time of the year, he ought to be able to reach his destination in just under six or seven weeks. Well before the winter freeze set in. If Gilbert delayed too long and Foster couldn't foist this investigation onto someone else, he might miss his window of opportunity to return to Canada.

Then too there was the risk of compromising Miss Daisy Alcott. That near kiss hadn't been to silence her as he had tried to tell her. It had been born of long held and ignored feelings for the lovely young woman. Feelings he had no right to after having left her to drown as a girl, as she liked to point out whenever she had the opportunity. He had no right to feelings for any woman until he could lay claim to a home for her, he reminded himself. It was just that Daisy was particularly unacceptable, considering she hated him.

But he would allow himself to admire her intelligence and tenacity from a distance. And then he would absent himself before he had to watch her wed with someone else.

Foster ignored his disappointment as she drifted away from his side and sidled up to Lord Simmons. Foster himself had advised the girl that Simmons would be a good match for her. It was idiotic of him to resent that now. Daisy deserved a good husband who would set her up well.

But when she proceeded to trounce her opponent at billiards and her gaze seemed to instinctively seek out his, Foster didn't deny himself the sense of satisfaction that generated within his organs.

"What are you glowering about?"

Foster turned with a grin toward his sister-in-law, still surprised and pleased to find he quite enjoyed having one of those. Really two of those, he corrected himself.

"You are doing a great job as hostess, Amelia."

"I know I am," she promptly replied with a light laugh. "But complimenting me isn't going to get you out of answering my question."

"I'm not glowering," Foster answered immediately, not trying to pretend he hadn't heard the question.

Amelia sighed. "You were," she insisted. "And it was in the direction of my very good friend, so I don't think I can allow for that behaviour."

Foster laughed. "What do you intend to do about it, even if it were true?"

"I could send you to your room without supper," she said with another light laugh even as she studied him with the speculation that could only arise from having many siblings. Foster tried not to squirm under her investigation. "You still haven't answered my question," she observed cheerfully. "I have the feeling your glower was aimed at Daisy. Or rather, Miss Alcott. You aren't about to become unpleasant, are you?"

"Why would you think I might become unpleasant? Am I not your favorite brother-in-law?"

Amelia stared at him with a frown. "No, I am of the opinion that Roderick is my favourite."

Foster laughed. "That's just because he's still at school so you are under the mistaken view that you can control him."

Amelia didn't contradict him but did join him in laughter. "Seriously, though, Foster. I would sincerely appreciate it if you would try to have a good time. And try very hard not to glare at my good friend."

"I've known her longer than you have. I have more knowledge that she deserves to be glared at."

Amusement filled him as he watched his hostess open and close her mouth as though trying to come up with a response but not sure exactly how to counter his argument. Finally, she smiled and patted him on the arm.

"I'm going to trust that you will behave like the gentleman you were raised to be and not cause a dreadful scandal that will offend all my guests."

It took all his concerted effort not to roar with laughter at that convoluted statement. "I promise you most sincerely that I will do my best not to offend all your guests. I cannot guarantee I won't offend Daisy, though, as she decided at a young age that I am most offensive to her. But that is her choice and not something you need to concern yourself about."

"It's far too late for that, Foster. I am already concerned. But as I mentioned, I am trying to trust you."

Foster suspected she was gritting her teeth as she said it, but she didn't say anything else, merely nodding to him and then walking away. It was interesting that she immediately went to confront Daisy. She ought to have tried harder not to make it obvious, but Foster assured himself that no one else was watching her quite as closely as he was. Except maybe his oldest brother, who clearly doted on his wife.

It was both heartwarming and revolting. Foster grinned at his own confused thoughts.

Seeing one's older brother so deeply in love was a disquieting experience. He was happy for Lucian, of course. He quite liked Amelia. But Lucian had always been almost angry and always domineering amongst his brothers. This new, happy, in love brother was a sight to behold and quite an adjustment to get used to. Lucian even seemed prepared to discuss feelings. It was not an offer he was prepared to accept from his brother, but it was an interesting thought to consider. Foster was fully aware that it was a change wrought by Amelia and her constant meddling. Even the old earl was more cheerful, which seemed like an impossible task if anyone had ever thought to ask Foster his opinion on the topic.

Lord Everleigh presided over Amelia's house party as though he had planned it himself, sitting at the head of the table at every meal and smiling over the assembled guests. Smiling. It was very odd. Foster couldn't remember seeing his father smile before. He had never given it a great deal of thought but if Foster had been asked, he would have said his father didn't know how. But whenever Amelia was in the room, it seemed both Foster's brother and his father couldn't help the reflex.

Still, seeing the old house he'd grown up in to be full of light and laughter wasn't something he minded in the least, even if it didn't feel like his home. It did feel welcoming for all the changes Amelia had introduced.

Cleanliness for one thing. Foster wouldn't have noticed it when he was younger but after learning to care for himself, he was more aware of the need to keep things clean, and it was the first thing he had noticed when he'd stepped foot in Everleigh upon his return this time. It smelled differently and felt fresh. Not something he could remember from his boyhood but was certainly something he was sure the permanent residents of the house were appreciative of. Except perhaps the servants charged with making those changes, he thought as he watched his sister-in-law manage the room with her usual determination and skill.

He hadn't been at Everleigh for long, but he had certainly enjoyed watching Amelia in action. And he greatly enjoyed seeing his father's delight in her company, too. The old earl should have remarried after the death of his wife, his sons' mother. Foster would never have thought to accuse his father of sentimentality, but that was the only explanation he could think of as to why the old codger had never remarried. Foster could remember how happy their family was when his mother was alive. There was a clear demarcation in his young life when his mother had died.

But seeing how happy his father was just having daughters-in-law told Foster the House should have had a mistress long ago. Not that it was his place to criticize his father's choices. How was he to know since he didn't even have a wife, yet let alone any children?

Foster pulled himself from the roundabout thoughts and tried to engage himself in the house party activities that were flowing around him. It didn't seem that Daisy was in the least bit distracted by their discovery that morning. She was laughing and flirting and chattering away as though she hadn't a single other thought in her head. If he hadn't witnessed her single-minded determination to discover what was in the cave, he wouldn't have believed she was even aware of a single thing other than the current game she was engaged in.

Watching her caused the oddest sensation deep in the pit of his stomach. She was the most engaging female he could remember encountering in his entire life. But it was as though she were dancing just out of his reach, like a mirage or a mist drifting on the wind in front of him.

He would walk into a room just to hear the tail of her laughter as she exited on the arm of Lord Merton or she danced onto the terrace with Lord Simmons or she tucked her hand into the elbow of Lady Constance and the two women put their heads together to exchange some bits of gossip.

It was maddening, and he wanted it to stop.

There was very little he could do about it and knew himself for a fool.

Foster found himself out on the back lawn with a bow in his hand, the arrow notched perfectly, and sighting down toward the target. Drawing a deep breath, he willed all other thoughts from his head even as he offered up a word of thanks that he could finally find an activity that would draw his full concentration. But just as he was about to release what was surely to be a bullseye, Daisy's lilting laughter drifted toward him from the maze into which she had wandered earlier.

Blessedly no one was nearby to be injured, but Foster's arrow did not reach the center of the target by any means. His cheekbones itched from the heat rising into them as he fought against the embarrassment that threatened to swamp his equilibrium.

Caroline came to his side with a frown.

"Are you unwell, Frost?"

Foster grinned at his brother's wife. "In a manner of speaking," he answered her, causing her frown to deepen.

"Can I help you with anything?"

"Do you know when Gilbert will be back?"

"I thought you would know," she answered, her frown deepening. "I haven't heard from him today."

"I haven't heard from him since I got here, so that's more than I've had from him."

"Oh dear, I'm sorry, Foster. I thought he was sending messages to everyone. Perhaps he expected me to keep you apprised. He is on his way but was delayed."

"I see." Even though he was disappointed not to have exact information, knowing Gilbert was on his way took a load off Foster's mind. He could soon hand the entire matter over to the one who ought to have been looking into it from the beginning. Foster could leave this house party and his maddening fellow guests soon.

The thought should have provided him with far more relief than it did. And Caroline's watchful gaze did nothing to lessen his chagrin.

"Was there something wrong with your arrow, Foster? I was expecting you to be the marksman to beat."

"I would have expected so as well," he agreed without rancor. "Perhaps I ought to try again. It's possible the arrow was faulty." Foster was proud of himself for managing to say that with a straight face.

"Carry on," Caroline answered with laughter in her voice and raised eyebrows, letting him know she wasn't being fooled by his attempts to prevaricate.

Foster knew she would be keeping an eye on him, and it would make it all the harder to find out what was going on at the caves. With Daisy there, he hadn't explored as much as he would have wished to. He needed to ensure there weren't other caves filled with illegally procured items. As a businessman himself, he understood the struggle of deciding between your desire to be honest and your wish to not overpay the government. But he also was well aware of the position illegally imported items put other businesses. As Daisy had pointed out, bringing cotton into the country without paying the exorbitant taxes the government demanded made life more difficult for the small tenant farmers who were trying their hand at cotton production. And their friend Lord Richmond who was just starting to grow the less sturdy product.

Cotton was new to their shores and the government was being surprisingly supportive by not taxing so heavily the product that was grown within the country. Which was probably why it was becoming an increasingly popular item to bring in illegally, especially with the ever growing popularity of velvet. How would you distinguish between local and foreign cotton once it was far from the coast? Scientists might be able to do so. Maybe even the ever-intelligent Miss Alcott would figure out a way, but Foster was reasonably certain no government tax agents would be putting in the effort to determine the difference. It would become a problem for the government and the small producers alike.

Foster sighted down his arrow once more. Practicing the art of archery would help him clear his mind of all its clutter if he could just ignore his single-minded attention on one Miss Alcott. He took a deep breath, held it, and then slowly released it as he also released the arrow. It flew straight and true, directly into the center of the target that had been set up.

"Bravo, Mr. Northcott!" The gathered guests who had been watching applauded his efforts and ability. But he couldn't hear them above the satisfaction of seeing Daisy's approving face nodding at him across the field. He turned his back on her. He didn't need this, he insisted to himself. There were far too many obstacles, not the least of which was her desire to have an uncomplicated future. His was certainly far from that, even if he had already reached his goals.

It would be best if he could leave this house party immediately, whether that offended his sisters-in-law or not. He couldn't do that, but he would be on a ship at the earliest possible opportunity. But he couldn't just leave his family's lands unattended.

Frustration welled within him. He should never have followed his sentimental urge to come home. It wasn't home, and his brothers weren't even all there. Lucian was far too busy with estate business to spend very much time with him, and everyone else was gone. He might as well write letters from the other side of the ocean as from Everleigh. He shook his head but still managed to smile at Caroline as she came to retrieve the bow from him.

"It would seem that previous arrow had been faulty after all," she declared with a grin and a giggle. "Here I was thinking you were distracted by the females in the group, but I should have known you better than that."

Foster wasn't completely sure if she was being droll or if she was sincere, but it didn't really matter. He would will her words to be true. He would no longer be distracted by anyone or anything. He would investigate the smuggling ring and then he would leave. He would do it all as discretely as possible so as to not offend

Amelia or Caroline, but he couldn't remain there much longer or he was sure to lose his mind.

"What do you have planned next for our entertainment, my dear?" he asked Caroline as she fell into step beside him.

"This isn't my show, Foster, I'm merely here to support Amelia," she began, as though admonishing him, but then she continued, "But I think she was planning for everyone to rotate through the activities that have already been set forward – the archery, exploring the maze, and croquet is set up on the other lawn. I don't think you've tried your hand at that yet, have you?"

"I have not," he replied promptly. "Thank you for the directions."

Chapter Eleven

D aisy was trying very hard to have a good time.

Well aware that her friends had gone to a good deal of effort in order for her to enjoy the house party, Daisy felt badly about how very distracted she was. She couldn't seem to enjoy Lord Simmons' attentions or even those of the very handsome Lord Merton. Both gentlemen seemed to be exerting a great deal of effort to charm her and she *was* charmed, she insisted to herself. But her head wasn't getting turned in the least.

Frustration was warring within her. She wanted to be caught by one of these gentlemen. It was exactly what she wanted for her life. A simple, uncomplicated, respectable life. Not one of high drama and deep emotion. She would save her deepest emotions for the babes she was sure to have in the years to come. She didn't need a love match. She didn't *want* a love match. She didn't want anything to do with the confusing swirl of conflicting emotions that would surely come with a deeply emotional connection with her husband.

Just take, for example, that dreadful swirl that had welled within her when Foster had nearly kissed her. She didn't believe him for a minute that it was to keep her quiet. Surely, he had been able to see as clearly as she had that the cave was empty save for the bundles in the corner.

Cotton. That was one more thing she needed to worry about. What if it was dangerous? She hadn't been paying a great deal of attention, but she had heard Amelia worrying about her brother-in-law's crops and that some sort of bug or something might have gotten into them. Daisy was reasonably sure she had meant it was something they could catch from another plant, much like she had caught her sister's cold.

They ought to be telling someone about those bundles. But who? And how to do it without compromising herself? Or could she just leave the matter in Foster's hands as he had tried to insist? Everything in her rebelled at that thought for innumerable reasons, not the least of which was that she didn't trust him.

Except that she *did* trust him. Deep down, instinctively. Which was ridiculous, considering she hated him, and he had left her to drown that one time. Perhaps he was right, and she ought to have forgiven him for that by now. They had been children at the time, even he was barely grown when it had happened, never mind the fact that he never ceased to appear burdened by it whenever she brought it up. But now there was that almost kiss to fret about.

Why couldn't she stop thinking about that?

Her gaze drifted to Lord Simmons' lips and there wasn't the least bit of fluttering in her midsection at the thought of him pressing them to her own. Unlike the entire flock of butterflies that had taken roost in her midsection when Foster had been near.

Daisy did her very best not to sigh over the inequity of it all. She was in the presence of the most suitable man for her needs and all she could think about was the least suitable. Why was she such a contrarian?

"Have you tried the archery yet?" Daisy wasn't even sure what his lordship had been talking about before, and she was probably being dreadfully rude to the poor, pleasant man, but her brain wouldn't work properly, and she couldn't sit there and pretend it would. If she couldn't keep Foster out of her mind, she might as well see what he was up to. He would probably need her assistance.

"I have tried my hand at archery in the past but not here at Everleigh." Lord Simmons didn't even seem upset over her turn of the subject, which was a distracted relief to Daisy as she was already on her feet and heading in that direction. "Have you done so?"

"No," Daisy replied with a smile. "My mother thought it unladylike. But she thinks Lady Adelaide is the perfect specimen of womanhood, so if she has proposed the activity, I am surely allowed to try my skills at it."

"I am sure you will be a natural."

Daisy blinked at that statement. "Really? Why?"

It was now Lord Simmons' turn to appear nonplussed by her. "You seem to be graceful and skilled at everything you try your hand at, Miss Alcott. I have no reason to think archery would be any different."

Daisy frowned for a moment, but then she offered him the sunniest smile she could manage. "That is quite the nicest compliment I have ever been given, I think, my lord. Thank you ever so much."

Light pink briefly visited the viscount's cheeks, and he appeared like a bashful schoolboy for the blink of an eye before he returned to his usual stoic self. For a moment, Daisy wondered if there might be more to the gentleman than she had at first thought, but she dismissed it as immaterial. She wanted a Society marriage. It was exactly right for her. If she could just get Foster off on his way back to the colonies, she would be perfectly set, she was sure of it.

"Since you know how to do it, perhaps you could show me," Daisy encouraged the gentleman at her side, adding to the hue of colour on his face.

"It would be my pleasure," he replied in a mild tone, belied by the pleased expression on his face. Daisy hid her smile. It wouldn't do to appear too sure of the outcome of the interaction. She ought to confer with her mother, although she was certain that everyone present for the house party was perfectly acceptable and eligible, since she wasn't looking for a love match, she ought to ensure it was the wisest decision she could make.

As they walked back out of the maze and toward the lawn where the target was set, Daisy thought to question the viscount a little. "Could you please remind me where your estate is, my lord? I am afraid if I'm not actually looking at a map when someone tells me where something is, the direction will not stick in my head."

"That is understandable, my dear lady, although I'm surprised to hear you mention maps. Do you look at them often?"

Daisy hesitated. She didn't want to turn his attention off her by seeming to be a bluestocking. She truly wasn't, despite her thirst for knowledge. She was quite a traditional girl if you could ignore her strong opinions on some things. So, the viscount needn't be concerned about her. And really, the potential mother of his future children ought to have some sort of a brain in her head, shouldn't she? But how to answer the question?

"Probably not often as compared to someone who actually travels," she finally began. "But I do find them fascinating. I'll never forget the first time my father showed me where we lived on the map in relation to

London and other notable places. I've been interested ever since."

"So, can you read a map?" he probed deeper, bringing a frown to crease Daisy's forehead.

"My apologies, my lord, but I'm not completely certain of your meaning. Do you mean, can I determine how far away something is from looking at a map? If that is your question, then I suppose the answer would be maybe," she concluded with a light laugh. "Since not all maps are accurate, and I'm not skilled or experienced enough to be able to tell if it's a good one or not, then I can't really answer the question. If it's a good map with an accurate legend, then yes, I can read it and tell where to go and how far away places are. Or I can in theory. I have never actually found myself with a situation where I was called upon to do so." She paused for a minute and looked at him carefully, wondering what exactly he thought of her answer but frustratingly unable to tell from his blandly pleasant expression. "What about you, my lord? Have you ever found yourself in a position of needing to rely upon your ability to read a map?"

"I have, actually, and you are quite correct about maps not all being reliable."

"Oh dear, did you have quite an adventure? I would love to hear about it."

"Perhaps another day," he replied, but Daisy suspected he was pleased with her question. "Come along, let us see how you do with the bow."

After showing her how to stand and demonstrating the proper way to hold the bow, Lord Simmons handed it to her. Daisy was a little uncomfortable with the crowd that had gathered to watch. She would rather not have an audience in case she turned out to be dreadful at it. But, as the viscount had said, she seemed to be able to do most other things, so how could this be much different?

Pulling back on the arrow, though, Daisy knew it was to be very different. She would have thought she was quite strong for her size given the various activities she participated in like riding and gardening. But it was going to take as much strength as she could muster to pull the string back far enough to make the arrow fly. She bit her lip and looked at the viscount through her lashes.

"Do you suppose I could maybe get a little closer to the target? Is that cheating? I don't think I'm going to be able to shoot that far."

"While I don't think we could say it's cheating, since this is just a game and not a competition, I think you'll be surprised by your own abilities. Give it a try first. If you really can't, then we'll move closer."

Daisy wrinkled her nose. She had thought the man would agree. Her eyes met Foster's watchful gaze, surprised to find it so firmly focused upon her. It crossed her mind that he would have let her approach the target. Or maybe he wouldn't have because, for him, everything was a competition. That thought made her smile and also lent strength to her muscles. She pulled back on the string as hard as she possibly could. Her aim wobbled, but she valiantly tried her best, letting the arrow fly.

It wasn't the truest aim ever, but her arrow actually overshot the target, much to her immense surprise. She managed to control the urge to turn and look at Foster for his reaction, but Lord Simmons' praise was sufficient to bolster her confidence.

"Try again, now that you've gotten a feel for it. And this time, try to line up where you'd like it to go."

Daisy bit back her reaction. She shouldn't get defensive; he was merely trying to help. And she did as he had advised. She carefully lined up the arrow with her destination, trying to account for the need to aim higher than the actual target. But she took too long, and her arm began to ache. Finally, she let the arrow fly, hoping it went in approximately the right direction. She was thrilled when it did hit the target with a loud thwack. But since it wobbled on its way there, it didn't make a good hit, bouncing off and landing on the ground.

Daisy handed the bow to Lord Simmons. "That was harder than I had expected," she admitted. "If I try again, I'm afraid my arm will be too tired for anything else. Why don't you try?"

The viscount seemed pleased with her for some strange reason. Daisy surmised that he was relieved that she wasn't an expert at archery but was a good enough sport not to make a fuss about it. With three brothers, Daisy was familiar enough with their thought processes to know a gentleman wouldn't appreciate her being an expert in anything, really.

But she found herself wondering what Foster had thought of it. He was different enough from most men that it was entirely possible he would have wanted her to keep trying. But it didn't matter in this instance. If she was going to return to the caves to investigate the smuggling efforts, as her confounded curiosity was insisting she do, she would need the full use of all her limbs. While the archery attempt was diverting, Daisy couldn't risk losing the use of her arms due to their overexertion.

She praised Lord Simmons' efforts along with everyone else who was watching and then she left his side to join her friend Amelia.

"You did well," Amelia complimented as she neared.

"Not really," Daisy said as she threaded her arm through her friend's elbow. "But it was a decent first try. I didn't get to see you do it. Did you hit the target?"

"Not from the distance you did."

Daisy's chin dropped down and her laugh sounded strained. "So, you could go closer? Lord Simmons indicated that it wouldn't be right to do so."

Amelia laughed with her but shrugged. "He was obviously trying to see how strong you are. I was impressed with your abilities, as was everyone else, I'm sure."

"I should have waited to see other ladies try," Daisy grumbled. "If I had known it wasn't cheating, I would have done much better."

"You did wonderfully well, especially for your first try. But I was surprised you didn't keep trying."

Daisy grinned. "I was afraid I would be maimed. It was hard!" They strolled along in companionable silence for a time before Daisy whispered to her friend. "Are you impatient for the little one's arrival?"

"You aren't supposed to talk about it aloud, Daisy Alcott."

Daisy rolled her eyes. "Amelia, don't be daft. I'm unwed but not stupid. My sisters have children, and I was raised in the country. I'm reasonably sure everyone here knows that eating too many bonbons makes a person grow in a much different manner."

To Daisy's surprise, her friend blushed to her roots and then grinned. "I am desperately impatient. That was part of the reason for this party. It gave me something to do. It also made you come for a visit."

"You could have just invited me."

"But you are determined to be wed this Season. I thought I could help you along and get what I wanted at the same time. Do you think it is working?"

"I'm uncertain, to be honest. You chose your guests well. It would seem both prospective gentlemen are willing to show an interest in me. Could I ask why you chose them specifically?"

Amelia wrinkled her nose at her friend.

"What exactly are you fishing for?"

"This is a spectacularly huge decision. You found a highly eligible gentleman and chose to fall in love with him. I don't wish to do that same thing. I just want the eligible gentleman, not the love part. So, I want the most eligible choice. It's hard to decide."

"I see. So, you don't actually have a preference, is that what you mean?"

They wandered off discussing the matter. Amelia didn't agree with Daisy's wish not to marry for love, but she didn't try to argue her out of it.

From what Daisy could tell, Amelia had chosen the wealthiest and most personable gentlemen of her acquaintance in her first attempt at making a match for her friend. Daisy was honored if not elated. She appreciated her friend's efforts.

Chapter Twelve

Foster couldn't get the interlude with Daisy in the cove out of his mind. Her question about who they ought to tell had been a good one, but it had been surprisingly difficult to find out who the magistrates in the area were. It seemed to Foster that there were many people in league with the gang of smugglers. Not that it really mattered. He had finally received a letter from his brother, and now that Gilbert was on his way home, Foster could safely leave the matter in his much more capable hands.

He had managed to gather some information his brother may or may not already know, namely who the local magistrates were. Squire Harris was one. And if that good man didn't feel fully qualified, Baron Strathmore in the next county was known to be just in his dealings with matters other magistrates didn't feel qualified to handle.

Foster wondered if either of the gentlemen would be able to truly handle the matter though. Depending on how big the smuggling ring turned out to be, it might be something they would need to involve agents from the king. Of course, that was where Gilbert came in, Foster supposed. And it was just as he was starting to despair about his brother ever arriving that he had finally received his brother's message that he would arrive the next day.

While running successful investments required what he thought was a great deal of brain power and negotiating skills, besides the ability to avoid criminals and those who wished you harm, Foster wasn't ashamed to admit that he didn't have what it took to be an agent or an investigator. He was looking forward to welcoming his brother, an actual agent for the Crown, home to Eveleigh so Gilbert could take over the investigation.

He was even more pleased to know that Gilbert was bringing customs officers with him to assist, much to Amelia and Caroline's dismay. Foster wasn't completely certain what they were worried about unless it was concern over their numbers not adding up anymore. Or perhaps it was wondering if they ought to be entertained at all. It was entirely possible the officers weren't of sufficient *ton* to be acceptable at the house party, in which case they could just be left to the grooms and other servants to entertain. When they weren't aiding in taking down the smugglers, that was.

In the meantime, while he awaited their arrival, Foster divided himself between trying his best to be a good guest for his new sisters and trying to find out as much as he could about who in the neighbourhood might be involved in the smuggling gang.

He was decidedly unused to subterfuge and the servants he had spoken to had invariably become skittish when he started asking questions. Foster couldn't decide if it had anything to do with their being involved or if it was because his father was their employer. Through his investigation, Foster began suspecting everyone and he could almost forgive Daisy for having thought *he* was up to no good with the way he was viewing everyone. Of course, she had gone about dealing with her suspicions in entirely the wrong way, but still, he could sort of understand.

Daisy's brother, Florent, had finally turned up to join Amelia's house party and for a moment, when he had caught his first glimpse of the man, Foster suspected he might be one of the men he and Daisy had seen climbing out of the boat that first night. But rather than looking shifty eyed or eager to leave, Foster thought he might have become instantly smitten with one of Amelia's female guests.

Lady Constance didn't seem to mind Florent Alcott's attentions from what Foster could see and hear.

"My lord, it has been a long time since we've met."

"I've heard you have been traipsing about all over creation."

Lady Constance shrugged. "There isn't much else for a woman to do."

Foster's eyebrows reached his hairline. What was she saying? And to Florent of all people? The most adventurous female in the Kingdom flirting with the least interesting gentleman? But Foster didn't have time to get sidetracked. No matter how curious he was about the sight of his old friend attempting a strange flirtation with the evasive, controversial young woman who couldn't be bothered to wait until she was a spinster to take up her independent life, Foster needed to maintain his focus on keeping an eye on the smugglers until Gilbert arrived with reinforcements.

Except, before he could carry on about this necessary business, his eyes caught on the sight of Daisy, also observing her brother and Lady Constance. He wasn't sure exactly what he was witnessing on her face, but he wished he could examine it a little longer. Or take her with him, he thought, before quickly dismissing the notion. The last thing he needed right then, when he was close to getting away from the mayhem, was to court trouble by involving himself even more with Daisy than he already had.

Despite that thought, though, he dithered a little longer to see what else Florent and Constance might have to say to each other. Lady Alcott joined the gathering crowd along with her crony Lady Bathurst. Foster again searched Daisy's face, wondering what she was making of her mother's sudden close friendship with the other matron at the house party.

With a final glance at the gathered guests, Foster made good his escape. He needed to follow up with his questions in the village, trying to identify who was tied up with the smugglers. He wanted to have as much information as possible before Gilbert's arrival so he could hand the entire sorry mess over to him and be done with it.

As he traipsed about the village, for the next day and a half, gathering a picture of fear that had begun to permeate the townspeople, Foster had trouble keeping Daisy from his thoughts. She had always been the most enticing creature he had encountered. Even when she was a child and he a schoolboy. Perhaps it was because he had lost his mother at a young age and had no sisters. But Foster knew it was more than that since Daisy's sisters had never interested him. There was just something about Daisy Alcott even when she was furious with him.

He couldn't be thinking of that right now.

He ought to be searching for the shack the innkeeper had described where he *might* find someone who could *possibly* know something that *might* help him discover who could *maybe* be involved in the cotton trade.

With a sigh Foster sank down onto a rough stool outside the blacksmith's barn. He was exhausted. As an adventurer and a businessman, he was used to things being much more straightforward. Oh, of course he had encountered unscrupulous dealers and liars and such. He knew not everything was straightforward. In fact, very little was actually straightforward in business. But it had never been as convoluted as this venture. He had never had such difficulty getting a truthful, honest, or direct answer from anyone before.

It was all the more difficult when all he really wanted to do was remain back at Everleigh watching over Daisy and getting to know his new sisters-in-law. He growled low in his throat, not much caring that he sounded more like an animal than a gentleman. Daisy was not for him. And his sisters-in-law would surely appreciate the safety that his investigating might bring them, even if they were never to know of it. If he had some real information to share with Gilbert when he finally arrived, they would be all that much closer to ridding their county of the gang of thieves that were surely in league with the smugglers.

But he was beginning to feel like a dog chasing its tail. Getting absolutely nowhere fast. He never did find the mysterious shack the innkeeper had described. Foster trudged in the direction of Everleigh feeling as though he had wasted an entire day of the precious few he had.

Chapter Thirteen

Daisy knew she shouldn't have come long before she got to the beach and realized the water was rising. But she had to know if the cotton was still there or if anything else had been added. She hadn't come in the night, having the sense to realize that would be taking this thing much too far. She didn't want to risk her life or her freedom. But she also couldn't let the matter lie.

She was also strangely unsettled watching her brother's flirtation with Lady Constance. It seemed their attraction had been instant and mutual. Why were everyone's lives advancing but hers? She didn't want to be jealous but she couldn't help it. It was a strange comfort to feel she had this secret adventure of knowing about the cotton in the cave.

It was to be a free afternoon for the house guests to do as they wished. Thankfully there were enough of them that Daisy was confident she wouldn't be missed. She would be able to imply to everyone that she had been with the others. It would allow her time to get to the caves, explore, and get back with no one the wiser.

Except the water was rising. There was a very real chance she was going to get wet. How was she going to explain that? Daisy dismissed the thought. It didn't matter. She would swear her maid to secrecy. It was the only chance she had of looking into the other caves. She would just have to be as quick as she could. And the rising tide might work in her favour. It was likely the smugglers were far smarter than she was and kept track of the tides better than she had. So, they would know about the rising water and were unlikely to be present. It was the safest time for her to be there. Well, apart from the actual water, but Daisy hoped to be fast enough that she could keep those old memories at bay.

"What are you doing here?"

Daisy heaved a frustrated sigh. Foster's presence wasn't going to help her forget about that long ago disaster.

"I'm checking on the safety of my home."

"No, what you're doing is being completely daft, Daisy. Don't you realize these are dangerous people?"

"The blunderbuss in their hands that night did give me that impression, yes, Foster, I am aware."

"Then I repeat my question, what are you doing here? You should be riding into the village to shop for ribbons or some such frippery."

"I don't have time for fripperies. You ought to have done that if that is your inclination. I needed to check on this," she waved her hands wildly toward the evidence of more activity in the cave.

"Why didn't you leave it to me to look after?"

"You didn't indicate that you were going to do so."

"Really, Daisy? You thought I would see smugglers on my father's land and just ignore the matter?"

Daisy shrugged. "Did you think I was to assume you would know what to do about them?"

"Yes," he nearly shouted at her, which perversely made her laugh.

"Well, I didn't. I wanted to see for myself just how serious a situation this might be. So, I'm here to see if there has been more movement. I thought if there was nothing here, maybe they'd taken it and moved on. Or perhaps I had dreamt the entire scenario."

"And what of my being here?" Foster's voice dropped an octave. "Have I been playing a part in your dreams often?"

"Don't be an idiot, Foster," Daisy scoffed despite the truth in his words. She would rather cut off her tongue than admit how much a role he played in her thoughts regularly.

She was relieved to see that Foster had a lantern with him. She snatched it from the ground and started exploring, surprised to see that the cave extended much farther back into the cliff than she had thought. The urge to explore was strong. Holding the lamp aloft and crouching down to see better, Daisy could see the cave branched off into multiple directions. She was sure to become quite lost if she wasn't careful.

"Don't go haring off in a wild pursuit, Daisy. The water is rising, and you are sure to run into trouble. You shouldn't even be here."

"It's not up to you to tell me what to do," Daisy insisted, even though she didn't fully disagree with him. "You should have told me you were coming to see for yourself."

"If I had, you would have insisted on accompanying me. I was trying to spare you the experience."

Daisy laughed, unable to contradict him.

"What do you intend to do now?"

"Now I will hand this mess over to one of my brothers. It is time for me to go home."

Daisy was buffeted by conflicting feelings. Turning hot and then cold, she wondered if she were coming down with some dreadful disease. Perhaps there was bad air here in the caves. The thought niggled at her mind while she fought against her delight and dejection over his departure.

"I thought *this* was your home," she commented.

"Just as Alcott is your home?" he asked softly, making her eyes inexplicably well with tears. She dismissed the softness that was threatening to goo up her insides. She was at Everleigh for a purpose that she meant to conclude in the wisest manner possible.

"So where are you off to this time?" she asked, ignoring the question he had countered hers with.

"I need to return to Upper Canada."

"Won't it be winter when you get there?"

"It will soon be, which is why I'd like to get going as soon as possible. The crossing should still be favorable for a while yet."

"Did you accomplish what you had intended by coming home?"

"Well, I've met my new sisters, so yes, you could say I have done so. I also had some business to take care of in London which is well under way."

"Will you be back again?"

"Someday," he answered softly, his hand lifting as though to reach toward her, but then he seemed to think better of the impulse.

"Have you chosen between Merton and Simmons?" he asked, his voice hardening in a manner that made Daisy think her answer might anger him. This brought a rising anger in return from her.

"It really isn't any of your concern, now is it, Mr. Northcott? You shall soon be halfway across the Atlantic. What those of us you leave behind choose to do with ourselves shouldn't even cross your mind."

"I would still like to know you will be happy."

"Of course, I'll be happy," Daisy countered immediately before softening. "Will you be happy in Canada?"

Foster shrugged. "I'll be doing something. That makes me happy."

Daisy nodded as though she understood. And for the most part, she did. She too wanted action. She wanted to stop dithering about her life. She needed to feel that she was moving forward. In a certain way, she supposed it was probably even stronger for a man. Foster must feel the need to provide for himself since no one had done so for him. At least ladies have a dowry arranged for them and usually a husband provided as well. Gentlemen often needed to fend for themselves, just as Foster was doing and her brother Reed was trying to do. It increased her curiosity about why Foster was there in the caves with her.

"Are you absolutely certain you had nothing to do with the placement of those bundles, Mr. Northcott?"

"Are you back to thinking I'm a smuggler, Miss Alcott?" Foster's voice was filled with incredulity. Daisy was relieved to hear there was no anger there with it.

"Not really, but it is most curious that you are here once more."

"No more so than your being here. In fact, far less than your being here. This is my family's land."

"Let's not have the same conversation as before. I've already expressed myself about my family's lands being nearly here, too. Besides, the tenants and everyone who would be affected. But you're right, I know you aren't involved. If it had been the brandy I had originally thought it to be, I would be far less likely to dismiss you as a possible party. But I don't see you as a cotton smuggler."

Foster laughed. "What do you suppose a cotton smuggler looks like?"

"Well, evidently we saw some for ourselves the other night."

Foster laughed again but looked around. "I don't think we're going to be able to investigate any further today. Our timing is dreadful."

"You have been here longer than I have, did you see anything in any of the other caves? That was what I had intended to do, search for more information."

"Can't you hear the waves coming in? There's no time for these questions, we need to get out of here."

"But I haven't looked," Daisy insisted.

"Don't be a fool," Foster snarled, turning her to force her to confront the waves.

Daisy stiffened instantly. She had chosen to ignore the rising danger. Fear flooded her just as the rising water was flooding the mouth of the cave.

"You're going to leave me to drown once more, aren't you, Frost? Only this time, there won't be someone else to save me." Her voice was growing increasingly shrill with each word she uttered.

"Daisy, stop it this minute. Driving yourself mad isn't going to help you in this moment. You and I both know that you are perfectly capable of getting yourself out of here. I am here and I will help you if you need it, but I know you can do this."

"No, I cannot. You are a dastard and I hate you."

Daisy knew she was being completely irrational, but she couldn't stem the ugly words that were erupting from her throat, seemingly of their own volition. From the clenching of Foster's jaw, Daisy surmised that he was seriously considering slapping her face to bring her to her senses. Daisy wondered if that might be the best plan because she was barely holding it together.

After Foster had ignored her pleas to save the kittens when they were children, Daisy had jumped in the lake to save them herself. But she hadn't realized how very heavy her clothes would become once they were wet. She also had forgotten that she didn't know how to swim. After Florent had pulled her from the lake and then boxed her ears for being so foolish, he had insisted that she learn to swim. So Foster was correct when he said she would be able to save herself. Except that she was not wearing a swimming costume. She was fully clothed in a day gown, a spencer, and all the various underthings a woman required for proper Society dress. And then there were boots and stockings and everything else. They would all weigh her down if she were forced to swim out of the cave.

She could, of course, remove her clothing. That would avert the disaster of the overweighted clothing. But then there was the little matter of how to return to the house without proper attire and without creating the biggest scandal the county had ever witnessed. Hysteria flooded her once more.

As though he could read her mind, Foster started unbuttoning her spencer. Daisy's eyes widened to the size of saucers, and she slapped away his hands.

"What are you doing?" she demanded.

"The water is rising too quickly. There is a good chance we'll have to swim. I was there, too, Daisy. I know what will happen if you try to swim in all your clothes. If you take some of them off now, you can carry them above your head. If you can get out before it's so deep you have to swim, you'll still have your clothes to cover yourself in order to return to the house."

He wasn't wrong. She took over the exercise of removing her outerwear. She also thought to remove some of her underthings. They were most likely to become heavy with water.

"Could you please turn around? Better yet, why don't you leave now? I will follow you when I'm ready."

"I'm not leaving you here. If you become hysterical, I'll bash you on the head and take you out unconscious."

Daisy laughed. "Would you really do that?"

"No, but hurry up," he nearly growled the words as he became more fed up with her dithering. But he did as she asked and turned his back to her so she could remove more of her clothes.

Perhaps she was being foolish to strive for modesty now. He was going to see her at some point if he wouldn't leave her behind. She could never look him in the face again. Somehow her youthful grudge against him now felt like the most innocent of disagreements. Daisy would never be able to see Foster and not think of this dark moment.

"Couldn't we try to wait this out?" she thought to ask, even as she continued removing items of clothing.

"It takes six hours for the tide to turn. Even if it doesn't get high enough to cut off all the air, which I suspect it might not, considering the bundles appear dry, I don't think we can be gone that long and your absence not be noticed. If you're hoping to make a match with one of your suitors, I'm sure you have no desire to be found missing."

Daisy sighed as she decided she had lightened herself sufficiently and quickly tried to wrap everything together tidily. Foster turned and helped her, closing the bundle with the buttons of her spencer and handing it to her to carry before thinking better of it and reaching to take the bundle from her.

"No, it's my responsibility. I will carry it," Daisy insisted, independent in the extreme, as usual.

She heard and ignored his sigh of exasperation just before he settled his hand at the base of her spine causing her to stiffen even as she wished to melt into him. She was suffering through the most inappropriate of emotions at the very worst time.

"Come along, you foolish imp. We shall get through this come what may."

Daisy tried to fan the flames of her rage with Foster but she just couldn't manage it. She knew he was not the villain she had tried to paint him all these years and now other, even more complicated, feelings fought for supremacy.

"I want an uncomplicated life," Daisy commented, apropos of nothing, as he hurried her toward the lapping waves.

"I hope you can achieve that, my dear." Foster's calm voice was nearly condescending. Daisy wondered what he was thinking but didn't care to ask.

"I'm not your dear."

"No, but the other things I'm thinking of calling you are even less appropriate," he countered as he urged her into the water.

Daisy gasped deep gulps of air.

"Breathe normally, Daisy. You'll make yourself lightheaded for no reason if you breathe like that."

"I am breathing normally."

He ignored her protest, grabbed her bundle with one hand and one of her hands with his other, taking big strides into the water and pulling her with him. Somehow, she managed to keep her footing even though the water rose to her knees and then to her hips as they walked out into the surf. They had to duck down into the water to get out of the mouth of the cave. Daisy managed to keep her head above the water, so her hair remained dry, but the rest of her was soaked to the bones. It was challenging to keep her feet solidly under her as the waves threatened to overwhelm her in the water's rush to the shore. She hadn't thought a river would have such a tide, but she supposed it was because they were so close to its mouth.

"Don't let yourself get bashed against the rocks," Foster yelled to her as he pulled her to the left, back toward the beach where the trail up to the bluffs was found. The water was back down almost at her waist but the skirts she had kept on were weighing her down. And her feet were unused to stepping on rocks, as she had bundled her boots in with her clothes.

Foster put his arm around her and nearly hoisted her out of the water.

"I can manage, Frost. Put me down!"

"Why will you insist on refusing my help?"

"Because I'm determined to remain independent," she yelled back at him fiercely.

"You are a fool. You can never be independent; don't you realize that?"

"Well, as close to being as I can pretend," she retorted in a huff, making him chuckle even as he helped her regain her feet, but he grabbed her hand once more.

"Hurry, Daisy. You're going to catch your death. Neither of us should have been in that cave."

"What would you have done if I hadn't turned up?" she asked as her teeth began to chatter.

"I was just on my way out when you came in. I'd be halfway home by now," he commented in such a cheerful voice that Daisy thought about pushing him under the waves to silence his smugness.

"You should have done so. I certainly didn't need you."

"What would you have done if you were on your own? Have you forgotten that I also had the lantern?"

Daisy gasped and turned to look back toward the mouth of the cave, causing him to laugh again.

"You normally have your brains in order. What has gotten into you?" he asked her suddenly.

"Do you really think so?" she asked, pleased despite her determination to remain furious.

Foster sighed and allowed the subject to drift away as they finally strode out of the surf. He hurried her toward the shelter of the cliffs, anxious to get out of the wind that would quickly freeze them in their wet state. Daisy appreciated his solicitous behaviour. He really ought to wash his hands of her. She had been unforgivably foolish, even she had to admit it.

"You ought to get back to the house. It would be bad enough for one of us to be caught, but if we're both found to be missing, there will surely be talk."

"You cannot expect me to leave you," he exclaimed.

"Unless you wish to wed with me," she countered.

"Is that what you were hoping for?" he demanded.

"Go away, Foster, I beg of you." Daisy pleaded as she sat down on a rock and began the arduous task of trying to get dressed while soaking wet.

Chapter Fourteen

To his shame, Foster did as she had bade him. He didn't know what else to do. While the smugglers could return, it was unlikely since surely, they would be more aware of the water than he and Daisy had been.

"You needn't trouble yourself about this matter any longer, Daisy," Foster had assured her before he left. "Authorities are on their way." He knew she wanted to question him further but he had only reminded her to hurry back to the house to avoid scandal.

What a debacle, he sighed to himself as he climbed up to the ridge where his horse had remained tethered. If Daisy was quick enough, she just might be able to make it into the house undetected. But that big of a house with that many guests and servants milling about, it would be a close-run thing. He ought to help her and ensure she made it as quickly as possible. But at this point, Foster was confident that the best thing he could do for her was stay far enough away that they were not associated with one another. He only hoped she had the sense to claim she fell or something. Perhaps into a pond or a stream. There were plenty enough on the property. It was entirely possible that no one would believe the graceful Miss Alcott could possibly fall into a body of water but if she returned damp and disheveled, she would need a story of some sort.

Foster was well on his way but still wanted to turn back to check on her once more and to remind her of the need to concoct a believable explanation. But he resisted his instinctive inclinations. He needed to get far enough away from her that he was no longer feeling pulled into her orbit.

Roderick, Foster's youngest brother, fancied himself to be a scientist. He was always on about various forces like gravity and magnetic pull. Foster was beginning to understand the concept far more now from his own experience than from any explanation his brother had tried to form.

Perhaps he would be far enough away from her once he reached the furthest shores of the Atlantic Ocean. Or maybe she would write to him. Foster goaded his horse into a faster pace as soon as they got far enough away from the rocky terrain nearest the bluffs. He needed the speed of a good run to have any hope of outrunning his thoughts.

When he got back to his room, with only encountering a couple footmen who didn't seem to notice anything amiss with his attire, Foster heaved a sigh of relief. He could only hope that Daisy would be able to accomplish the same feat.

A stack of correspondence awaited him on a small table in his room. The servants had been busy, he could see. All his things had been tidied so the stack of papers stood out and caught his attention. He was reluctant to turn his attention to business as his mind was firmly back on the beach, thoughts tangled up with Daisy, as always. But that had never happened to him in his life. He was always of a mind for business.

Foster sat down at the small desk and grabbed the first missive. Surely, he had a strong enough will to be able to force his thoughts to cooperate.

Minutes later he was deep in thought reading and rereading each item that had been sent to him.

He needed to return to his holdings in Upper Canada as soon as he could manage.

But he didn't need to return alone this time. He had done it. He had amassed his fortune. He could take a wife whenever he pleased. He pulled himself up short on that thought.

Perhaps he ought to go over there and verify for himself that he truly had struck it so rich in that particular mine. It was possible that it was one big deposit, not an actual vein of the stuff as the miners suspected. Besides, he needed to get there as quickly as possible to ensure the security was as good as he expected it to be. If he really had hit the load he thought might be there, there would certainly be much more interest in his property than there had ever been before. Its inaccessible and inhospitable atmosphere wouldn't be a deterrent forever.

And that was no place to take a wife, he reminded himself. Which aristocratic woman would willingly submit themselves to the deprivations of an ocean crossing and then the further journey to his properties, which would be even more arduous? And with winter approaching, it was sure to be a nightmare for most women. Except maybe Lady Constance. Or Daisy.

His breath caught in his throat. Could he marry Daisy Alcott? Would she have him? She had been professing to hate him for years. And he had left her to fend for herself on the beach. What woman would entrust herself to a cad who would do that? Even if it had been with reluctance? He hadn't wanted to risk a scandal that would force them to marry. And now he *hoped* she would marry him? All because he now had the finances he felt he needed to feel secure and wealthier than his brother. His younger brother? Why would he still be so immature as to be in competition with his brothers and yet have the temerity to expect an exceptional young woman like Daisy to accept his hand in marriage?

He wouldn't blame her if she refused. But he was glad she wouldn't be forced to accept. He cared enough about her to want her to have the choice. And she certainly had choices with the way the two visiting viscounts were acting toward her. Foster hadn't had the stomach to watch closely enough to be able to guess whether she would prefer Merton over Simmons. But he was going to try to convince her to pick him over anyone. He was suddenly swept with the absolute opposite of confidence. Despair was more like it. How was he going to convince her to attach her life to his?

He would have to remind her that she didn't actually want the staid, predictable life she was setting herself up for. That if she would give adventure a try, she would surely love it just as he did. That just as they both learned how to swim after that fateful summer day that tore them apart, they would both learn to do whatever they needed to in order to thrive in their life of adventure, only this time they would do it together.

Fear squeezed his insides. He wanted that life, but he didn't know if he could convince Daisy that she wanted it, too.

The other letter contained further details from his brother. Gilbert and the customs officers would arrive the next day. All his matters were getting tied up nicely. He had done what he had set out to do when he'd come to Everleigh. He had gotten to know his new sisters and while he hadn't discovered the identities of the smugglers, that wasn't his problem to solve. He had gathered enough information that he would be able to leave it to Gilbert to deal with the bounders. It was a relief that he wouldn't have to do it himself.

Foster quickly righted his appearance before going off in search of the women in his life. He needed to speak with his sisters and with Daisy.

Chapter Fifteen

He had actually left her.

Daisy stared off into the distance, already fully exhausted and there was still the ride back to the House to get through. She was relieved that she at least had a horse to get her back this time. Not that she was completely certain how she was going to be able to get up onto said horse by herself. Especially not filthy and tired as she was. Daisy bit her lip. She was having an adventure. She ought to be much more delighted than she was.

But the matter of the smugglers still hadn't actually been resolved. She didn't know anything about it, really, aside from the fact that Foster claimed someone with authority would be taking over. That sounded quite lovely. She wished she could make everything else go away that easily. She was always claiming she wanted to be independent and make her own choices in life but in that moment, she wished someone would arrange it all for her. Right now, she wanted to be back at Alcott House, or perhaps even their London townhouse, and for this to all be just a strange dream.

If she could open her eyes and it be late morning in her room in London, her maid bringing her morning chocolate and selecting the appropriate gown for strolling in Hyde Park, that would be such a relief.

But would it really? Daisy realized she wouldn't have wanted to miss out on this experience even if it had been difficult and slightly terrifying. It wasn't even quite over. She had to get back to her room without anyone questioning her too deeply as to her absence or her appearance.

It was unlikely Lord Merton would take a hoyden for his wife. Neither would Lord Simmons, even for all his seeming charm and delight in her turn of phrase and skill at sports. They were all on the right side of respectable. Daisy doubted even that kind gentleman would be able to turn an accepting eye onto this particular adventure. Nearly being flooded into a cave with Foster Northcott and removing half her clothes in order to escape with her life if the worst had happened and she had lost her footing.

But she hadn't lost her footing. Foster had kept her safe. The exact thing he hadn't done when they were children. Daisy knew she would have to stop hating him now. But if she didn't hate him, she was afraid the feelings would be just as fierce but far stronger. And that was not the life she wanted. She wanted to feel secure. She mostly liked predictable. Or she rather thought she did. She didn't really like those delicious flutters of emotion that being near Foster tended to cause. And if she didn't hate him anymore, there was no way to know what sort of sensations there would be. Surely far more than a true lady could bear.

Having felt those flutters, though — and she was willing to finally admit to herself she hadn't hated them — could she in fact settle for the independent Society life she had wished for? Was she willing to give up her independence? That was the actual question she faced. Not that it really mattered, she reminded herself as she rode toward Everleigh House after finding a stump to assister her in climbing onto her horse. Foster had left her, after all. Surely, he wasn't contemplating wedded bliss with her. And she certainly didn't want him through force. She needed to ensure she got back to her room without incident. She didn't have any desire to be painted with the brush of scandal.

If Foster didn't want her, she certainly didn't want him to be made to have her and in the meantime, there were two fine gentlemen seemingly vying for her attention. In a rather lukewarm manner, but still, they were demonstrating at least a modicum of interest in courting her.

Daisy rolled her eyes and groaned. Just days ago, that was exactly the situation she claimed to wish for. Even yesterday, if pressed, she would have said she was delighted to finally have two perfectly acceptable and boring viscounts to choose from. It was hard for her to believe that she had actually convinced herself that she wished for boring. What was wrong with her? What could have possibly made her think that she would be happy with boring?

Foster.

He was the question and the answer every time.

But he had left her to fend for herself.

It was at her demand, it was true, but what proper man would leave a lady to fend for herself?

Daisy rode along, not bothering to hurry, deep in thought, pondering that very question.

A man who trusted that the young woman in question was perfectly capable of looking after herself, that's who would leave her behind. Of course, there were others who would do so as well. Cad-like men, of which she knew Foster was not. But Daisy was certain that neither Viscount Merton nor Lord Simmons would be willing to leave her behind like that. But it wasn't out of chivalry. Or maybe it was, but it was also out of an understanding that the little woman couldn't possibly look after herself in a perilous situation.

Daisy sighed. On one hand, that was probably lovely. But on the other, while she did appreciate help and support, she also wanted to be thought of as capable, able to look after matters if they needed looking after. Surely a man ought to be confident in the abilities of the mother of his future children.

But they probably did have confidence in her abilities of which they expected her to have. The expected types of things. Hostess duties, conversation, menu planning, staff management, and all the other necessary things that a viscountess ought to know how to do. But a simple Mrs. needed to know many more things, in Daisy's estimation. It was a rather thrilling thought.

A thought she would have to ignore completely for the rest of her days. As Foster had said, Ashford, his younger brother, wasn't coming back anytime soon, and Roderick was far too young and of the wrong sentimentality for her newfound purposes. And Foster himself hadn't expressed the least bit of interest in her, if one could ignore that near kiss in the cave.

She couldn't ignore it, of course, but she didn't place much stock in it. He hadn't actually finished it. Nor had he seemed inclined to repeat the experience. She supposed she had done it wrong. Or given him a disgust of her when she pushed him away.

Daisy grinned. She had reacted most strongly. But who could really blame her? She had never before been kissed; how was she supposed to know how it was done? Surely, he should have told her what he was doing. Oh, very well, she accepted in her thoughts. He had just been trying to keep her quiet, just as he had said. Another sigh escaped her.

Very well, she nodded. It was Lord Simmons for her. Foster wasn't the right one. He had his adventures in the New World to keep him occupied and she really didn't see herself traipsing all over the world, even if she were to be invited. Lord Simmons' estate wasn't over far from where her sister lived. That would be most convenient for visits and to make sure their children were close all through their lives.

Yes, Lord Simmons was the perfectly acceptable choice for her. Now she just had to avoid all hint of scandal and bat her eyelashes at him until he came up to scratch. Easy peasy.

The house came into her view, and relief and disappointment warred for dominance in her chest. She wanted to sob but managed to curb the impulse.

Of course, there was a flurry of activity as soon as she arrived in the stable yard. Grooms gathered around exclaiming over her having ridden out without one of them and someone ran to the house, presumably to set up a hue and a cry over her there. Daisy felt as though she were sunk.

But it was Amelia who arrived on the scene and set it all to rights, leading Daisy away like a lost child, eager for the scold that would mean she was safe.

"What have you gotten yourself up to, Daisy? You look quite a mess."

"Would you believe I fell in the pond?"

"No, I would not believe that. You wouldn't go anywhere near it; that is why there isn't a single activity planned this week near that thing. Tell me what's really going on."

"What makes you think something's going on? I just wanted some quiet, and I love these parts."

"I know you, silly. I know something is afoot. And for some strange reason I suspect it involves Foster. I find that decidedly hard to believe, but Caroline is convinced of it as well. She would have come with me but we wanted to prevent scandal, so she is keeping everyone else occupied while I see to you."

"I do not require seeing to. I am perfectly capable of getting myself tidied up without an escort, thank you."

"But you forget that I cannot allow shenanigans under my roof."

Daisy burst into laughter even though she suspected Amelia might be quite serious with her words. But Daisy couldn't watch her friend's attempt at severity with a straight face.

"Amelia, my dear friend, I would throw my arms around you and squeeze you, but you are quite perfectly composed, and I most certainly am not. But please, do consider yourself embraced."

"Noted," Amelia said with a slight nod and an even slighter smile making it harder for Daisy to control her laughter even though she tried. They arrived at Daisy's room and Amelia swept her inside like the matron she now was. "Now, start talking. I can understand you not wanting to answer my questions in the hallway, as anyone could overhear, and I apologize for asking for those same reasons, but I will get answers now, and don't make me ask again."

"Or what? What are you leaving out here Ames? I went for a ride. Why is this so offensive to your sensibilities? I can assure you, there was nothing havey cavey about it at all."

"You never struck me as a liar before."

Daisy gasped and tears sprang to her eyes. Before they could fall, though, she was once again able to see the humour in the situation. "Very well, there was something cavey about it. I went to the beach with the caves and my timing was off. I had to step into the surf a little bit."

"Why would you do that? And then why would you try to claim a much different tale?"

"Because it turned out to be more dangerous than I expected and I didn't want anyone, including you, ringing a peel over me."

Amelia stared at her quite fiercely for a moment.

"Do I need to arrange a special license for you?"

Now it was Daisy's turn to stare. "Would you even know how if I did?"

Amelia's face melted into a smile. "I might not, but I'm certain Adelaide would."

"Keep your stomach-turning lovey nonsense to yourself. We aren't all thusly afflicted."

Amelia stared anew and sank down onto the bench at the end of Daisy's bed. "Now I know there's more to this than just a ride to the beach. What has gotten into you, and what do you have against love?"

"I don't want to feel it, Amelia, you know that. I just want to get on with having children and leading my life."

"Don't you think it would be better to love their father and be in a partnership with him?" Amelia was puzzled but trying to understand.

"I was hoping for a simple life on an estate where I could make a home with my children and live comfortably. I don't think involving so much emotion is going to be comfortable for me."

Amelia reached out, grabbed Daisy's hand, and pulled her down to the bench beside her. "My dear girl, you ought to seek much more than merely comfortable. Forming a love match leads to the highest heights of joy."

"But what if he doesn't love you back or he betrays you in some way? Or what about when he dies?" Daisy's voice was rising, but she couldn't seem to help it. "I have been in mourning for most of the last couple of years, which is why I'm so late seeking my match. But that has really brought home to me that everyone dies."

"Well of course everyone dies, silly. But you're going to be sad about their death whether you were deeply in love with them or not, aren't you? Wouldn't it be better to be joyously happy in the meantime?"

Daisy stared at her friend. She had been absolutely certain that she didn't want such a relationship, but it was a delight to see Amelia and Lucian together this week. And even though Caroline's husband hadn't yet arrived, it was evident from the way Caroline spoke of him that she was in alt over their marriage. Daisy was happy for them, she truly was, but she was still hesitant to make such a match for herself.

"It's something to do with Foster, isn't it?" Amelia asked again, gently this time. "Something happened between the two of you when you were children that has never been resolved, I'm sure of it. But surely, it's time, Daisy. Whatever it was, you have to let it go. I think Foster could be a good match for you, but if you cannot forgive him for that past hurt, at least let it go enough to find someone you *can* love. Just being comfortable should not be your life's goal."

Daisy grinned but it felt slightly lopsided. "You didn't answer my question about what if he doesn't love you back."

"I don't have an answer for that, I'm sorry to say. It's true that love is a risk. But I firmly believe that it is worth the risk. Have you not read any novels from the circulating library?"

This droll question brought them both to hysterical laughter, far more than was warranted, but it was the perfect release of the pent-up emotions.

"Come along and I'll play lady's maid. We need to get you cleaned up and back out into Society or your swains will come pounding on your door."

"You're determined to have a scandal on your hands, aren't you?"

"No," Amelia denied hotly. "I was just saying we need to get you out in order to avoid scandal."

"But you are seeing it in every chance encounter."

Amelia's expression turned sheepish. "It was the one thing I was terrified of, that having all these eligible men and women in my house would lead to different matches than I was hoping for."

"And here you thought that's what I was up to," Daisy realized. "I am truly sorry. There was nothing of the boy and girl variety about my excursion to the beach, I promise you."

"And yet you're still not really telling me why you have been going off exploring instead of playing along with the amusements I've arranged."

"I wasn't very good at archery," Daisy tried to excuse.

"You only tried twice," Amelia countered before she laughed. "Never mind, I'll get it out of you later. For now, we really do need to get you cleaned up and back out amongst the guests."

Amelia suited her words to actions, and Daisy was soon restored to being the presentable young maiden she was. But Daisy could see in her reflection as she tweaked a lock of hair just so, that her eyes were turbulent with questions she didn't have answers for. She could only hope that Foster had figured out what to do about the smugglers as he assured her he would. She didn't want to approach Lord Adelaide or his father about the criminals. She thought of telling her brother, but he would probably have even more questions than her hostess.

Daisy was still a tumult of emotions when Foster found her in a parlor later that afternoon.

"Could I interest you in a walk through the maze?" he asked her in a low tone that sent shivers through her. Daisy was reasonably sure that had not been his intention; he probably just didn't want to be overheard by anyone else in the room, but still, it carried the delicious scent of secrets, and Daisy couldn't resist.

"You could," she answered with a smile, rising to her feet, and taking his proffered arm.

"You managed to return to the house without incident. I must compliment you on your ingenuity," Foster said as they strolled across the lawns at a sedate pace.

"Don't be so quick to offer compliments. Amelia had set the servants to watching for me. The grooms clucked over me and ran for her as soon as they caught sight of me. You'd think I had abused the horse for the way the stable hands were going on."

"I'm sure it wasn't that. They were probably disgruntled that you didn't take one of them with you."

"Perhaps, but they were certainly quick about running for their mistress."

"That is understandable, surely. But what did Amelia say? Did she take you quite to task?"

"She was most peculiar, to be honest, and she promised to squeeze the details out of me later, but she was determined that I not cause a scandal so she wanted me restored to tidiness and back amongst the guests as quickly as possible, so she didn't lecture me too thoroughly. But she is convinced I'm up to something, possibly involving you." Amelia paused and shook her head with a light laugh. "I knew she was smart, but I didn't expect her to be that canny."

Foster laughed along with her. "I know what you mean. I've been avoiding her gaze for days because I feel as though she is about to pounce and torture me for details."

"Have you spoken to Adelaide about the smugglers? Do I need to? Or should I tell my brothers?"

"You needn't worry about it any longer. I have passed the information on to Gilbert, actually, who has just arrived, and the matter will be taken care of promptly."

"Gil? What does he have to say to anything?"

"If you promise to keep it a secret, I'll tell you."

Daisy laughed harder than was necessary, but it was probably the relief talking through her giddiness. "I'm not sure if I want any more secrets, but all right, I promise not to tell."

Foster lowered his face again and put his head closer to hers, even though there was no one anywhere close enough to hear them. It sent tingles through her, and she wasn't sure she would even be able to hear him over the buzzing that took up residence in her ears.

"Gil is an agent for the Home Office," he said in a deep, low voice, with glee evident in his tone as though his secret delighted him.

"No, I can hardly credit it," Daisy exclaimed. "Do you suppose Caroline knows?"

"I'm sure of it. In fact, I wouldn't put it past her to be an agent, too."

Daisy almost turned around to stare across the lawns in search of her friends. "Does Amelia know?"

"Don't look. Remember, you're supposed to be keeping it a secret," Foster admonished her.

Daisy giggled. "Foster Northcott, you are being utterly silly. No one can hear us. No one could possibly guess what we're talking about. And certainly no one would think any of them are agents."

"But you swore to secrecy."

"Very well, I apologize," she said, lowering her voice. "Do you think either of them have ever killed anyone?"

"Daisy Alcott, why would you ask a question like that?" he demanded making her laugh even harder.

"Because this is the most ridiculous conversation I could have ever imagined first thing this morning. But never mind, it doesn't matter. Do you trust that Gilbert will be able to do something about the smugglers?"

"I do. I would trust him anyway because he's my big brother, but I've been led to understand that he's actually a very good agent and has been for at least a few years."

Daisy's eyes rounded in surprise, and it took effort to prevent her chin from dropping down in response to the level of her shock. "I would never have guessed."

"I suppose that's the point," Foster replied with a grin. "Anyhow, all of that to say that neither of us need concern ourselves any longer."

Daisy hummed in thought. "Does it mean that I'm a candidate for Bedlam that I am somewhat disappointed?"

Foster did not react at all in the way she would have expected. His hand came up to settle over hers where it was tucked into the crook of his elbow, and he looked at her with his eyes aglow with a warmth she had never seen before. Suddenly he was hurrying her into the mouth of the maze. Before she could even understand where they were going, he had her pulled down a dead-end trail and sitting on a bench.

"Are you truly disappointed, Daisy?"

Heat coloured her cheeks. Why would he persist in that topic? She had mostly been funning. She lifted one shoulder in half a shrug, uncertain how to answer.

"Please allow me to rephrase. Why would you find it disappointing? Were you hoping to continue the investigation yourself? Or did you enjoy the excitement of having an adventure? Or was it perhaps the prospect of spending time with me?"

It seemed to Daisy as though her face were on fire, so great was her embarrassment. But she reminded herself that it was Foster even as she remembered Amelia's advice about a love match. Perhaps she ought to take a risk even if it meant the potential for hurt or embarrassment.

"Maybe a little bit of all those things," she said in a low voice that made it sound like a question rather than a statement, which seemed to please and amuse Foster. She was on the verge of taking offence at his amusement when he turned more fully toward her on the bench and took possession of both of her hands.

"Would you consider coming with me to Canada?"

For the second time in the space of a few minutes, Daisy's chin was again dropping down in shock.

"Come with you to Canada? But how?"

Now it was Foster's turn to blush. "I'm sorry, I'm doing this completely wrong." He sighed and fidgeted but didn't let go of her hands. "I meant to start with an apology. For leaving you this morning. And, I suppose, for almost killing you that time when we were children. I know you've had a hard time trying to forgive me, but I do hope you will. You see, I didn't know how to swim. And I never wanted to admit that to you because I loved having you follow me around so faithfully. But I was a foolish boy more interested in saving face than repairing our broken relationship, and then it was easier to just run away to the colonies."

Daisy laughed. "It was easier to run off to Canada than to admit you didn't know how to swim?"

"Pride is a ridiculous thing, isn't it?"

Daisy nodded. "I can relate. I didn't want to admit that I didn't know how to swim either. But Florent made me learn that very summer. He was furious that I would allow myself to get in that situation."

"How could he have thought it was your fault?"

"Well, I was the simpleton who jumped into the pond fully clothed without any idea how to rescue myself let alone the kittens I had jumped in to save."

"And you've been afraid to take risks ever since, haven't you?"

Daisy nodded, unable to meet his gaze, but he squeezed her hands tightly. She tried to be brave and returned her gaze to his face.

"But you've wanted to do so, haven't you, Daisy?" Foster prompted, still squeezing her hands.

Daisy shook her head a little. "Not until this week," she whispered. "Your being here seems to bring out the worst in me."

"It's not the worst, Daisy. It's the very best. I love your adventurous streak. And I love that you wanted to protect your family and the tenants. I love that you are such good friends with my new sisters. And I love that you didn't recoil with horror when I asked if you would consider coming with me to Canada."

Daisy blinked away the sheen of mist that wanted to cloud her vision. "That's a lot of things," she whispered.

"I love you, Daisy. I have stayed away from home because I didn't feel able to take a wife, and I didn't want to see you wed with someone else. Even though I have been an absolute dolt all these years, I think I have always loved you, ever since you were such a sweet little girl tagging along after your brothers and mine, even when I nearly killed you, the mistake I will regret for the rest of my life."

"You love me? But how do you know?"

Foster laughed with delight over her question. "I just know that my life will be greatly limited without you in it. I know that together we will be far greater than apart. I know that you will be the perfect partner to come with me and attend to the discovery that workers have made in one of my mines in Upper Canada, and then you will be the perfect companion to settle down in a house or cottage somewhere in the vicinity of Everleigh or Alcott and help me raise a couple of Northcott grandchildren." He pulled her closer, letting go of one of her hands in order to put his arm around her. "What do you say, Daisy? Can you keep the secret of our love and marry me?"

Daisy was nearly breathless with wonder and knew her eyes were bright and shining with unshed tears as she nodded in the affirmative. Apparently, Foster didn't need words as his head closed the gap between them and he sealed their agreement with his lips. Moments later, he thought to ask her one more important question.

"How angry will your mother be if we marry by special license so we can get to Canada before winter?"

Daisy gurgled with laughter.

"Not angry in the least. After already planning rather spectacular weddings for my two sisters and almost despairing of my wedding, she will be delighted, I'm certain. Especially if you allow her to assist in the acquisition of a home in the neighbourhood, unless you already have your eye on something."

"Nothing specific, but I had set an agent to the task of seeking out a property."

"Were you that sure of me, then?"

"Not at all, my darling, I wasn't sure of you in the least, merely hopeful. But I knew I didn't want to be so far away from my family any longer and thought it would be good to have a home in the vicinity one day. I didn't know I was going to be able to accomplish it so soon."

There was no further conversation for a time.

Epilogue

Florent Alcott was furious.

Not about his sister's betrothal. Not really. Foster Northcott was a fine fellow and he was almost certain the man was nearly worthy of his little sister. No, what had Florent nearly beside himself with anger was the fact that he hadn't noticed.

And it was all Lady Constance's fault.

That beautiful woman had somehow put a spell or some such nonsense upon him. There was surely no other explanation.

So, while he smiled and applauded and hopefully made all the appropriate gestures and noises of support for his sister who was nearly glowing with happiness, Florent was nursing a grudge against a beautiful young woman who had kept him from seeing what was right under his nose.

How had Foster courted Daisy without him noticing? Florent prided himself on knowing everything that was going on in his home and in his family. It was his personal rule for his own conduct. All things Alcott were his responsibility. And because of Lady Constance, Daisy had arranged her own match for herself.

Never mind that it was exactly what she had wanted to do. And he was actually very happy for her. But it wasn't supposed to happen without his knowledge.

Florent knew it was his pride that had been stung so he made every effort to swallow it down and beam with delight whenever the happy couple was near. Even when they announced they wished to wed by special license so Daisy could hare off to Canada with her soon to be husband.

The fond brother watched with a mixture of relief and dismay as Lady Adelaide took over all the arrangements, seemingly delighted that her house party had been such a success that it was to culminate in a wedding. He was relieved that he didn't have to make the arrangements as his mother didn't seem overly anxious to do it, but he was dismayed that he felt suddenly so out of his depth.

He hadn't even thought he was so fond of his sister but when Daisy had tucked her small hand into his elbow and looked up into his face with such a smile of joy, it was all Florent could do not to weep like a weaning infant.

"How did you grow up so fast, baby sister?"

Her soft chuckle told him all he needed to know. If Daisy didn't take offence over his question, she was truly smitten.

"Thank you for not kicking up a fuss," Daisy said with a grin.

"Why would I kick up a fuss?"

"Because you're the most proper Alcott there is," she said simply. "I'm sure you don't appreciate the suddenness of this turn of events."

"Is there something particularly scandalous about it?" Florent had to work at keeping his anger from her. It wasn't Daisy's fault he had been blinded. "Wedding a gentleman you've known all your life shouldn't surprise anyone, I wouldn't think."

"But you aren't anyone, Flor," Daisy pointed out.

Florent sighed and dismissed his anger. He would deal with it later. Right now was his sister's moment and he needed to give it to her. He wouldn't have many more of these interludes with her now.

"I will admit that it does feel sudden to me on one hand. But you have always had strong feelings toward Frost. I was quite convinced they were of the nature to prevent marriage. But anyone who looks at the two of you would have to admit it isn't fury holding you together."

Daisy grinned at her brother. "Not fury, no. Although there has been plenty of that through the years." She paused and Florent watched her gaze search out her betrothed. "I didn't think I craved adventure, but I am even looking forward to the crossing."

"That certainly surprises me."

Her gurgle of laughter rewarded his dry comment.

"Isn't it ridiculous. I thought I didn't want to experience love, but I find it is the most delightful lark."

"Are you absolutely certain of your decision, Daisy? I'll stand by you even if you've committed some atrocity."

She laughed again. "I swear to innocence, Flor, have no fear. And yes, I'm sure of my choice. I also swear we'll be back before you know it."

Florent raised his eyebrows at that statement and she revised it slightly. "All right, perhaps not so very quickly, but Frost promises we shall settle here or near abouts. We'd both prefer to be close to our families for the most part with only occasional ventures across the sea."

"I'd have thought you'd prefer to keep your feet on dry ground."

"I would have thought so, too," Daisy agreed with the sweetest smile her brother had ever seen grace her face. "But it turns out love does the strangest things to your brain."

Florent nodded and couldn't explain why his gaze suddenly sought out that of Lady Constance.

The End

- - - - - - - - - - - - -

Want to find out what happens with Florent and Constance?
Read the next book in the *Northcott Kinship* series:

Distracting the Heir

She was just trying to help another lady out...

The *Northcott Kinship* series is connected to the *Sherton Sisters*. Have you read those yet?
Start with Book 1

A Duke to Elude

She's waiting for true love. He's tasked with uncovering the truth. When nefarious schemes threaten her reputation, he finds his heart on the line with it.

About the Author

I learned to read when I was four or five, listening to my mother read to me when I was lonely after my brother started school. Ever since, I've had my head buried in books. I love words – historical plaques, signs, the cereal box – but my first love has always been novels.

A little over ten years ago my husband dared me to write a book instead of always reading them. I didn't think I'd be able to do it, but to my surprise I love writing. Those early efforts eventually became my first published book – Tempting the Earl (published by Avalon Books in 2010). It has been a thrilling adventure as I learned to navigate the world of publishing.

I believe firmly that everyone deserves a happily ever after. I want my readers to be able to escape from the everyday for a little while and feel upbeat and refreshed when they get to the end of my books.

When not reading or writing, I can be found traipsing around my neighbourhood or travelling the world with my favourite companion.

Stay in touch:

Website   Facebook   Instagram   TikTok

Stay in touch with Wendy May Andrews
and forthcoming publishing news.

Sign up for her biweekly newsletter

Other books by Wendy May Andrews:

Ladies of Mayfair

The Governess' Debut

The Debutante Bride

The Reluctant Debutante

Sweet Surrender

A Dangerous Debut

Mayfair Mayhem

The Duke Conspiracy

The Countess Intrigue

The Viscount Deception

The Bequest

Inheriting Trouble

Courting Intrigue

Inviting Misfortune

Sherton Sisters

A Duke to Elude

A Viscount to Conspire

A Lady to Reveal

A Gentleman to Avoid

A Sister to Beguile

Northcott Kinship

Assisting Lord Richmond

Evading the Gentleman

Intriguing Lord Adelaide

Distracting the Heir

Convincing Mr. Northcott

Orphan Train

Sophie

Cassie

Katie

Melanie

Married by Proxy

A Wife for Carter

A Wife for Ransom

A Wife for Alastair

A Wife for Hamilton

Dear Aunt Judy

Torn in Toronto

Singed in Saint John

If you like Regencies with a touch of adventure, you will love **the *Mayfair Mayhem* series. Book 1 is:**

Anything is possible with a spying debutante, a duke, and a conspiracy.

Growing up, Rose and Alex were the best of friends until their families became embroiled in a feud. Now, the Season is throwing them into each other's company. Despite the spark of attraction they might feel for one another, they each want very different things in life, besides needing to support their own family's side in the dispute.

Miss Rosamund Smythe is finding the Season to be a dead bore after spying with her father, a baron diplomat, in Vienna. She wants more out of life than just being some nobleman's wife. When she overhears a plot to entrap Alex into a marriage of convenience, her intrigue and some last vestige of loyalty causes them to overcome the feud.

His Grace, Alexander Milton, the Duke of Wrentham, wants a quiet life with a "proper" wife after his tumultuous childhood. His parents had fought viciously, lied often, and Alex had hated it all.

Rose's meddling puts her in danger. Alex will have to leave the simple peace he craves to claim a love he never could have imagined. Can they claim their happily ever after despite the turmoil?

Available now on <u>Amazon</u>

If you like Regency Romance, read:

Inheriting Trouble

Book 1 in *The Bequest Series*

The inheritance was meant to better her life, not muddle it.

Georgia Holton, wellborn but nearly penniless, is best friends with one of the Earl of Sherton's five daughters. When she is invited to accompany her friend for two weeks of the Season, Georgia jumps at the opportunity to have a little adventure away from her small village.

The Earl of Crossley is handsome, wealthy, widowed, and jaded. He has no intention of courting any of this Season's debutantes. After all, every woman he's ever known has been dishonest, including his late wife. But when a chance encounter throws him into contact with the Sherton ladies and their lovely friend, he can't help being drawn to Georgia's beauty and endearing personality.

When confusion about Georgia's small inheritance becomes known, a sense of obligation to right a wrong, forces the earl and Georgia into close association.

But is she really different from any of the other women, or does she have an ulterior motive?

And can Georgia even consider getting close to a man from High Society, when all she wants is to return to her simple village life?

Sparks fly between these two, but it will take forgiveness and understanding on both their parts to reach a happily ever after.

Available now on <u>Amazon</u>

Also enjoy this Sweet Regency Romance:

Book 1 in the *Sherton Sisters* series:

A Duke to Elude

She's waiting for true love.
He's tasked with uncovering the truth.
When nefarious schemes threaten her reputation, he
finds his heart on the line with it.

Lady Rosabel, eldest daughter of the Earl of Sherton, has no interest in being a Duchess, despite countless proposals from eligible nobility. Secretly, she is waiting for a love match—preferably with someone who carries no title. Bel's third Season is predictably disappointing until the mysterious Duke of Wexford arrives and has her questioning her plans to refuse any suitor with his status.

James Allingham, the 6th Duke of Wexford, seems to have inherited the role as advisor to the ailing King along with the dukedom. Investigating Lord Prescott's schemes is tricky enough without the interference of Lady Rosabel. She is beautiful and intelligent, but Wexford has no time for courting.

Wexford needs to uncover everything about Prescott's plans to destabilize the colonies. When Lady Rosabel is implicated in the schemes, James fights his suspicions of—and his attraction to—the beautiful young woman as he presses on to find the truth.

Discover the page-turning intrigue of this clean Regency romance today!

Available now on Amazon

Made in the USA
Middletown, DE
30 October 2023

41625967R00111